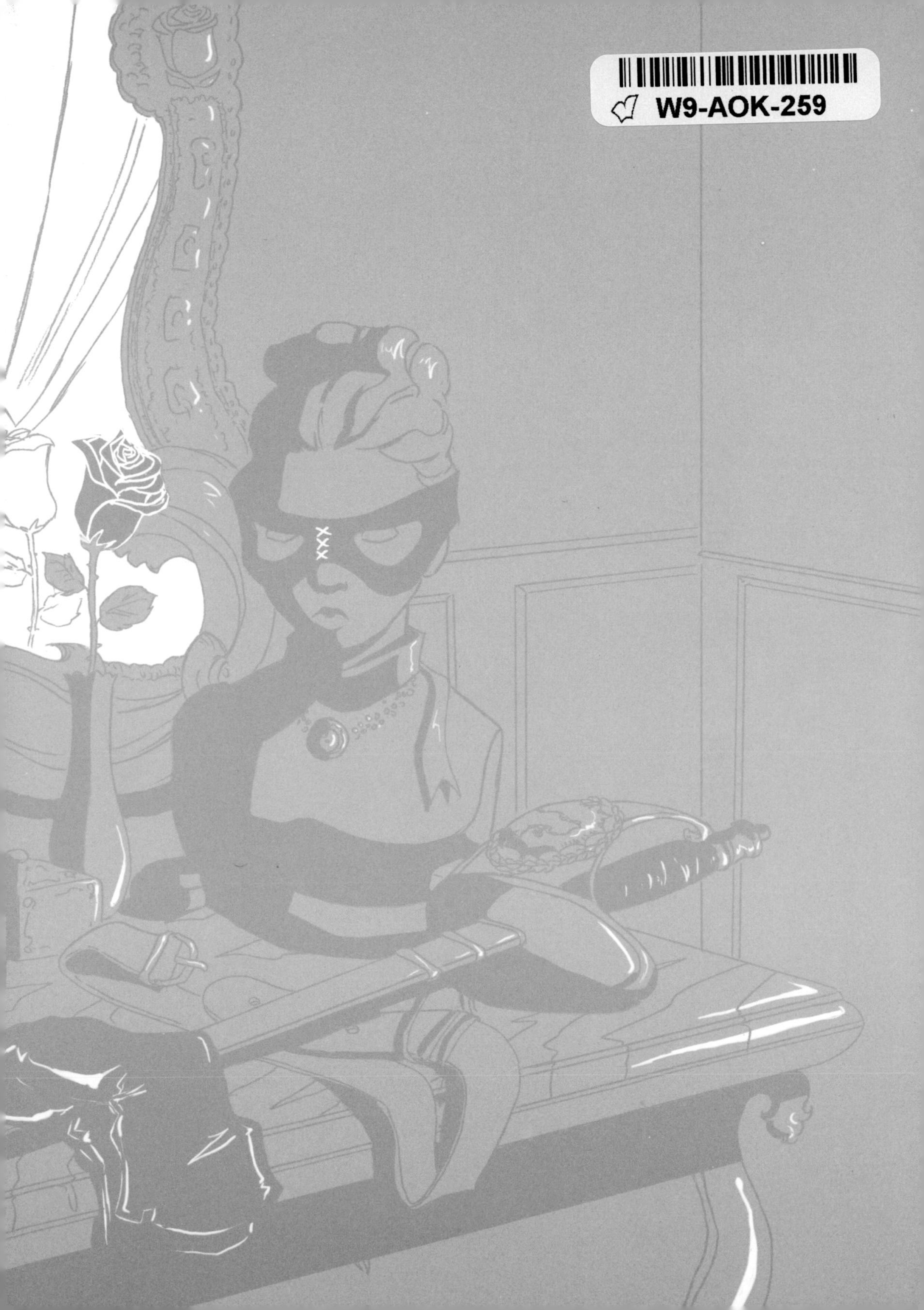

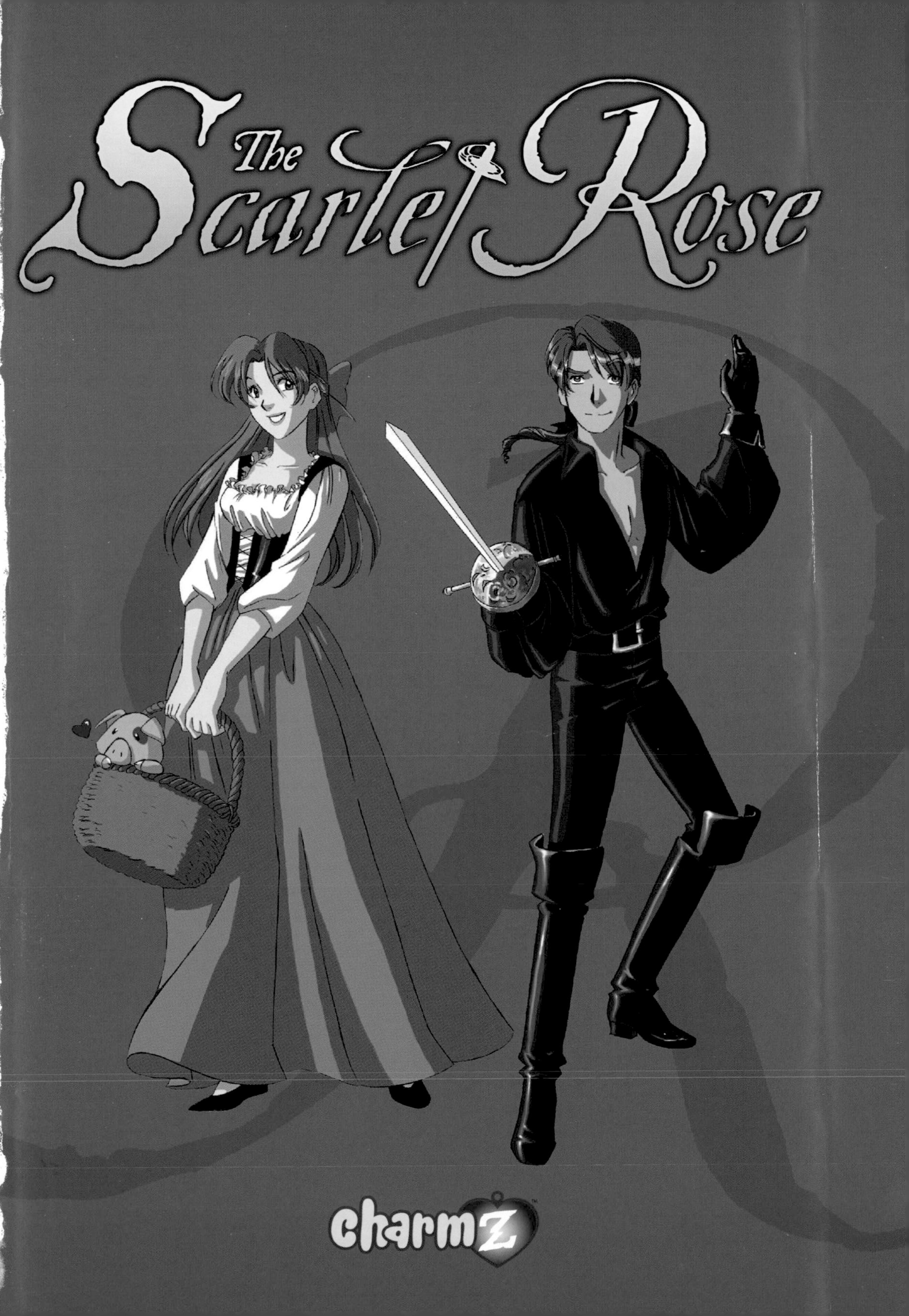
The Scarlet Rose
charmz

MORE GRAPHIC NOVELS AVAILABLE from Charmz™

COMING SOON!

STITCHED
MARIAH McCOURT
AARON ALEXOVICH
The First Day of the Rest of her Life
charmz

STITCHED #1
"THE FIRST DAY OF THE REST OF HER LIFE"

STITCHED
MARIAH McCOURT • AARON ALEXOVICH
Love in the Time of Assumption
charmz

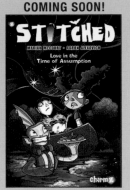

STITCHED #2
"LOVE IN THE TIME OF ASSUMPTION"

PATRICIA LYFOUNG
The Scarlet Rose
charmz

SCARLET ROSE #1
"I KNEW I'D MEET YOU"

PATRICIA LYFOUNG
The Scarlet Rose
I'll Go Where You Go
charmz

SCARLET ROSE #2
"I'LL GO WHERE YOU GO"

Greg Tessier and Amandine
Chloe
The New Girl
charmz

CHLOE #1
"THE NEW GIRL"

Greg Tessier and Amandine
Chloe
The Queen of High School
charmz

CHLOE #2
"THE QUEEN OF HIGH SCHOOL"

ALL-NEW Graphic Novel by Greg Tessier & Amandine
Chloe
Frenemies
charmz

CHLOE #3
"FRENEMIES"

Sweeties
CHERRY SKYE
charmz

SWEETIES #1
"CHERRY SKYE"

GFFs
GHOST FRIENDS FOREVER
charmz

G.F.F.s #1 "I LEFT MY HEART IN THE 90s"

Ana and the COSMIC RACE
AMY CHU
KATA KANE
THE RACE BEGINS
charmz

ANA AND THE COSMIC RACE #1
"THE RACE BEGINS"

Charmz graphic novels are available for $9.99 in paperback, and $14.99 in hardcover. Available from booksellers everywhere. You can also order online from www.papercutz.com. Or call 1-800-886-1223, Monday through Friday, 9–5 EST. MC, Visa, and AmEx accepted. To order by mail, please add $5.00 for postage and handling for first book ordered, $1.00 for each additional book and make check payable to NBM Publishing.
Send to: Charmz, 160 Broadway, Suite 700, East Wing, New York, NY 10038.

Charmz graphic novels are also available wherever e-books are sold.

The Scarlet Rose

"I'll Go Where You Go"

STORY & ART BY

PATRICIA LYFOUNG

COLOR BY

PHILIPPE OGAKI

NEW YORK

To Pelote, I love you, you little scamp.
To Joëlle.

Thanks to Hulya and Françoise for "loaning" Fanelli to me,
Thanks to Sevda for "loaning" Medusa to me.
Thanks to the readers of THE SCARLET ROSE.
Every day, your enthusiasm helps me continue this adventure.
To Pepito, the living room prince.
And finally, to Philippe, mi amor, I totally dig you!
–Patricia Lyfoung

The Scarlet Rose

By Patricia Lyfoung
La Rose Écarlate, volumes 3 and 4
Lyfoung © Éditions Delcourt-2007/2008
Originally Published in French as "J'irai où tu iras"
and "J'irai voir Venis."

English translation and all other editorial
material © 2018 by Papercutz.
All rights reserved.

THE SCARLET ROSE #2
"I'll Go Where You Go"

Story, art, and cover by Patricia Lyfoung
Color by Philippe Ogaki
Translation by Joe Johnson
Lettering by Bryan Senka

Spenser Nellis—Editorial Intern
Jeff Whitman – Assistant Managing Edtior
Jim Salicrup
Editor-in-Chief

PB ISBN: 978-1-62991-874-7
HC ISBN: 978-1-62991-875-4

Charmz is an imprint of Papercutz.

Chamz books may be purchased for business or promotional use.
For information on bulk purchases please contact Macmillan
Corporate and Premium Sales Department at
(800) 221-7945 x5442

Printed in India
April 2018

Distributed by Macmillan
First Charmz Printing

PREVIOUSLY IN *The Scarlet Rose* ...
After witnessing the murder of her blacksmith father, Jean-Baptiste de Laroche, eighteen year-old Maud moves to a country estate outside of Paris to live with her disapproving grandfather. Along the way she encounters The Fox, a masked Robin Hood–like rogue—a dashing figure she falls for. Her grandfather struggles to tame her wild spirit and introduce her to Society. He arranges for Guilhem de Landrey to be her fencing instructor hoping that might rein her in. Still seeking to avenge the murder of her father, with her new fencing skills, and inspired by the Fox, Maud becomes the masked avenger, The Scarlet Rose, much to the dismay of Count de Landrey. Fearing for Maud's safety, Guilhelm reveals his secret to her, that he is actually The Fox!

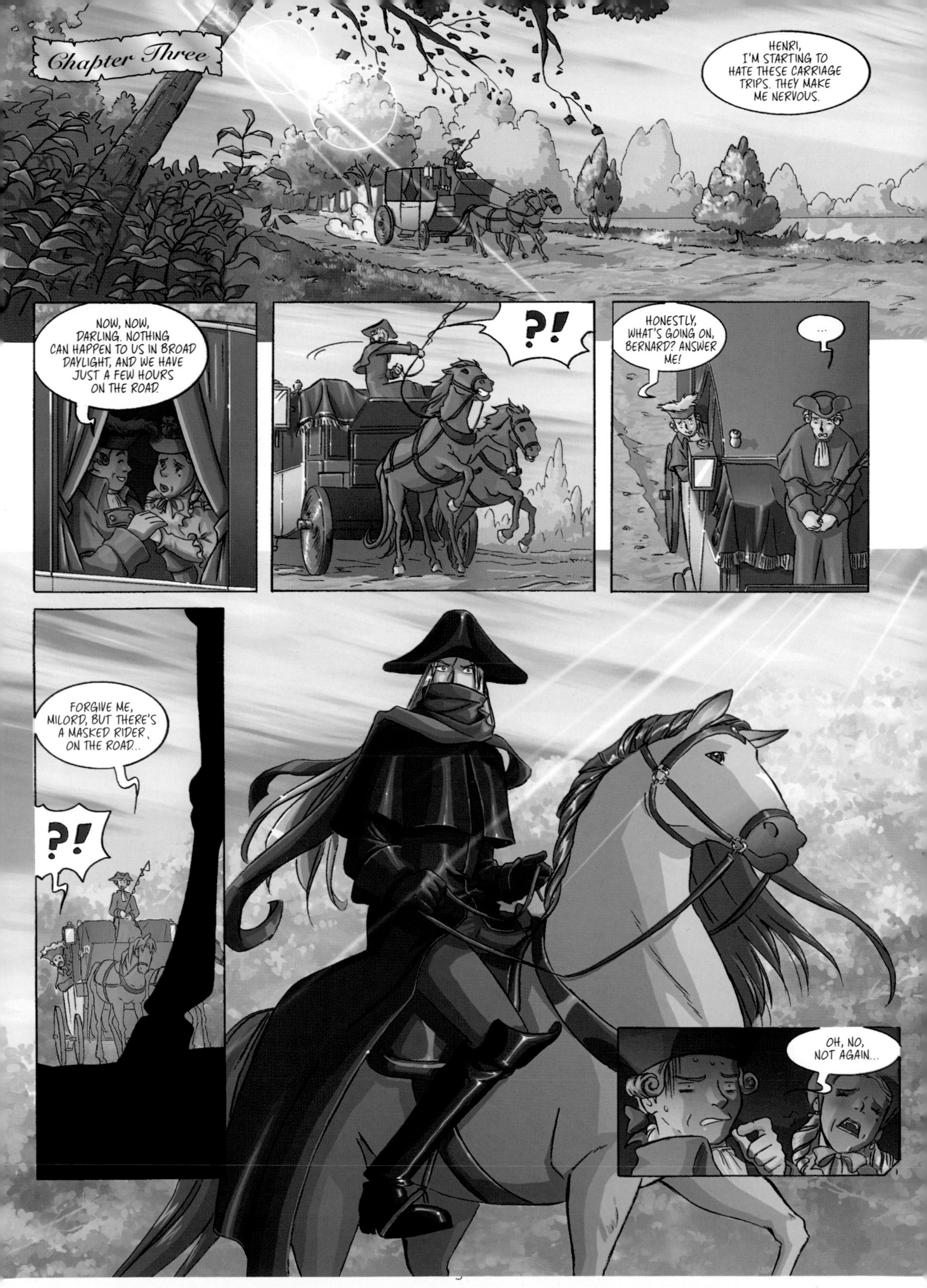
Chapter Three
HENRI, I'M STARTING TO HATE THESE CARRIAGE TRIPS. THEY MAKE ME NERVOUS.
NOW, NOW, DARLING. NOTHING CAN HAPPEN TO US IN BROAD DAYLIGHT, AND WE HAVE JUST A FEW HOURS ON THE ROAD.
?!
HONESTLY, WHAT'S GOING ON, BERNARD? ANSWER ME!
...
FORGIVE ME, MILORD, BUT THERE'S A MASKED RIDER ON THE ROAD...
?!
OH, NO, NOT AGAIN...

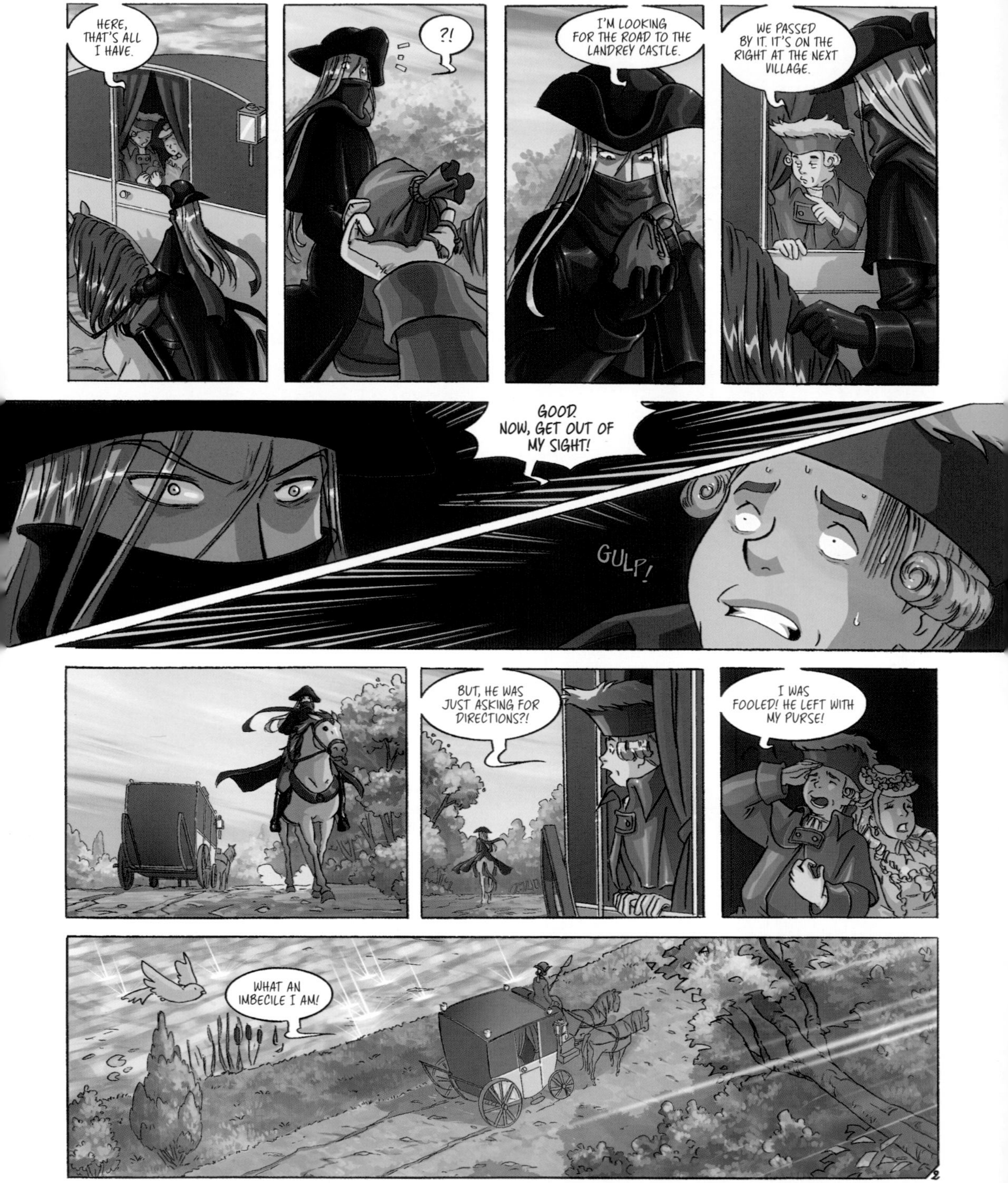
HERE, THAT'S ALL I HAVE.
?!
I'M LOOKING FOR THE ROAD TO THE LANDREY CASTLE.
WE PASSED BY IT. IT'S ON THE RIGHT AT THE NEXT VILLAGE.
GOOD. NOW, GET OUT OF MY SIGHT!
GULP!
BUT, HE WAS JUST ASKING FOR DIRECTIONS?!
I WAS FOOLED! HE LEFT WITH MY PURSE!
WHAT AN IMBECILE I AM!

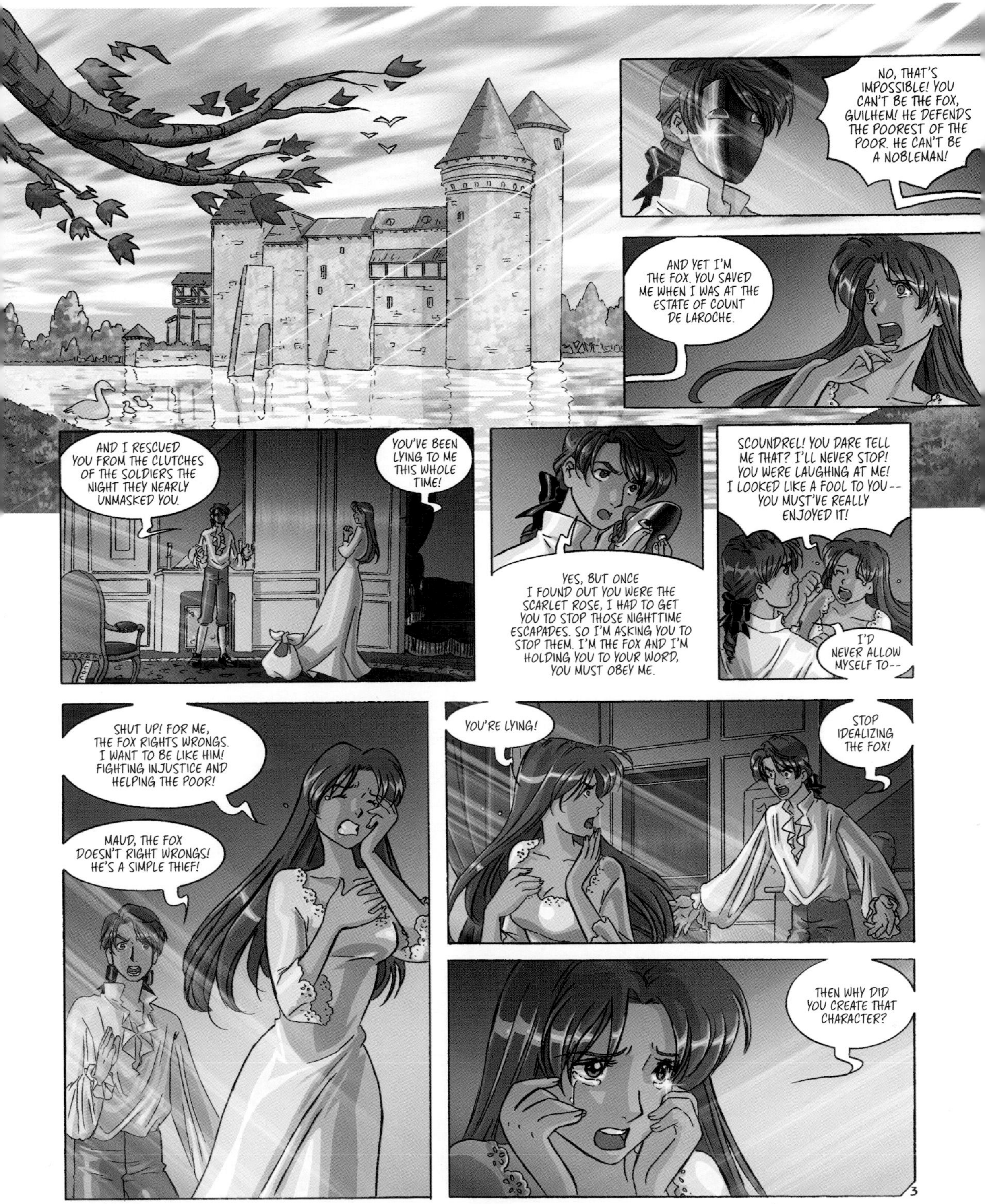
NO, THAT'S IMPOSSIBLE! YOU CAN'T BE THE FOX, GUILHEM! HE DEFENDS THE POOREST OF THE POOR. HE CAN'T BE A NOBLEMAN!
AND YET I'M THE FOX. YOU SAVED ME WHEN I WAS AT THE ESTATE OF COUNT DE LAROCHE.
AND I RESCUED YOU FROM THE CLUTCHES OF THE SOLDIERS THE NIGHT THEY NEARLY UNMASKED YOU.
YOU'VE BEEN LYING TO ME THIS WHOLE TIME!
YES, BUT ONCE I FOUND OUT YOU WERE THE SCARLET ROSE, I HAD TO GET YOU TO STOP THOSE NIGHTTIME ESCAPADES. SO I'M ASKING YOU TO STOP THEM. I'M THE FOX AND I'M HOLDING YOU TO YOUR WORD, YOU MUST OBEY ME.
SCOUNDREL! YOU DARE TELL ME THAT? I'LL NEVER STOP! YOU WERE LAUGHING AT ME! I LOOKED LIKE A FOOL TO YOU-- YOU MUST'VE REALLY ENJOYED IT!
I'D NEVER ALLOW MYSELF TO--
SHUT UP! FOR ME, THE FOX RIGHTS WRONGS. I WANT TO BE LIKE HIM! FIGHTING INJUSTICE AND HELPING THE POOR!
MAUD, THE FOX DOESN'T RIGHT WRONGS! HE'S A SIMPLE THIEF!
YOU'RE LYING!
STOP IDEALIZING THE FOX!
THEN WHY DID YOU CREATE THAT CHARACTER?
3

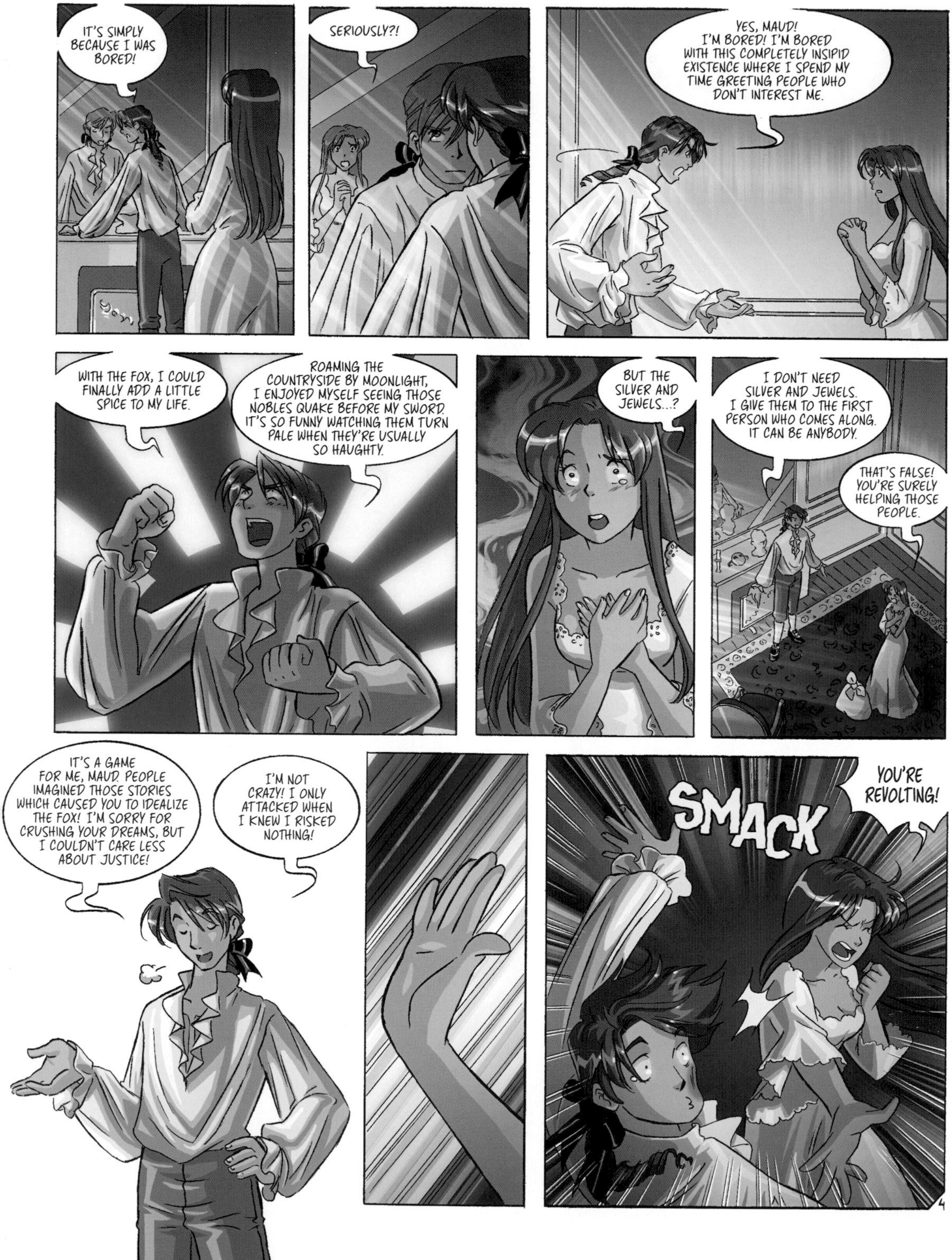
IT'S SIMPLY BECAUSE I WAS BORED!
SERIOUSLY?!
YES, MAUD! I'M BORED! I'M BORED WITH THIS COMPLETELY INSIPID EXISTENCE WHERE I SPEND MY TIME GREETING PEOPLE WHO DON'T INTEREST ME.
WITH THE FOX, I COULD FINALLY ADD A LITTLE SPICE TO MY LIFE.
ROAMING THE COUNTRYSIDE BY MOONLIGHT, I ENJOYED MYSELF SEEING THOSE NOBLES QUAKE BEFORE MY SWORD. IT'S SO FUNNY WATCHING THEM TURN PALE WHEN THEY'RE USUALLY SO HAUGHTY.
BUT THE SILVER AND JEWELS...?
I DON'T NEED SILVER AND JEWELS. I GIVE THEM TO THE FIRST PERSON WHO COMES ALONG. IT CAN BE ANYBODY.
THAT'S FALSE! YOU'RE SURELY HELPING THOSE PEOPLE.
IT'S A GAME FOR ME, MAUD. PEOPLE IMAGINED THOSE STORIES WHICH CAUSED YOU TO IDEALIZE THE FOX! I'M SORRY FOR CRUSHING YOUR DREAMS, BUT I COULDN'T CARE LESS ABOUT JUSTICE!
I'M NOT CRAZY! I ONLY ATTACKED WHEN I KNEW I RISKED NOTHING!
SMACK
YOU'RE REVOLTING!

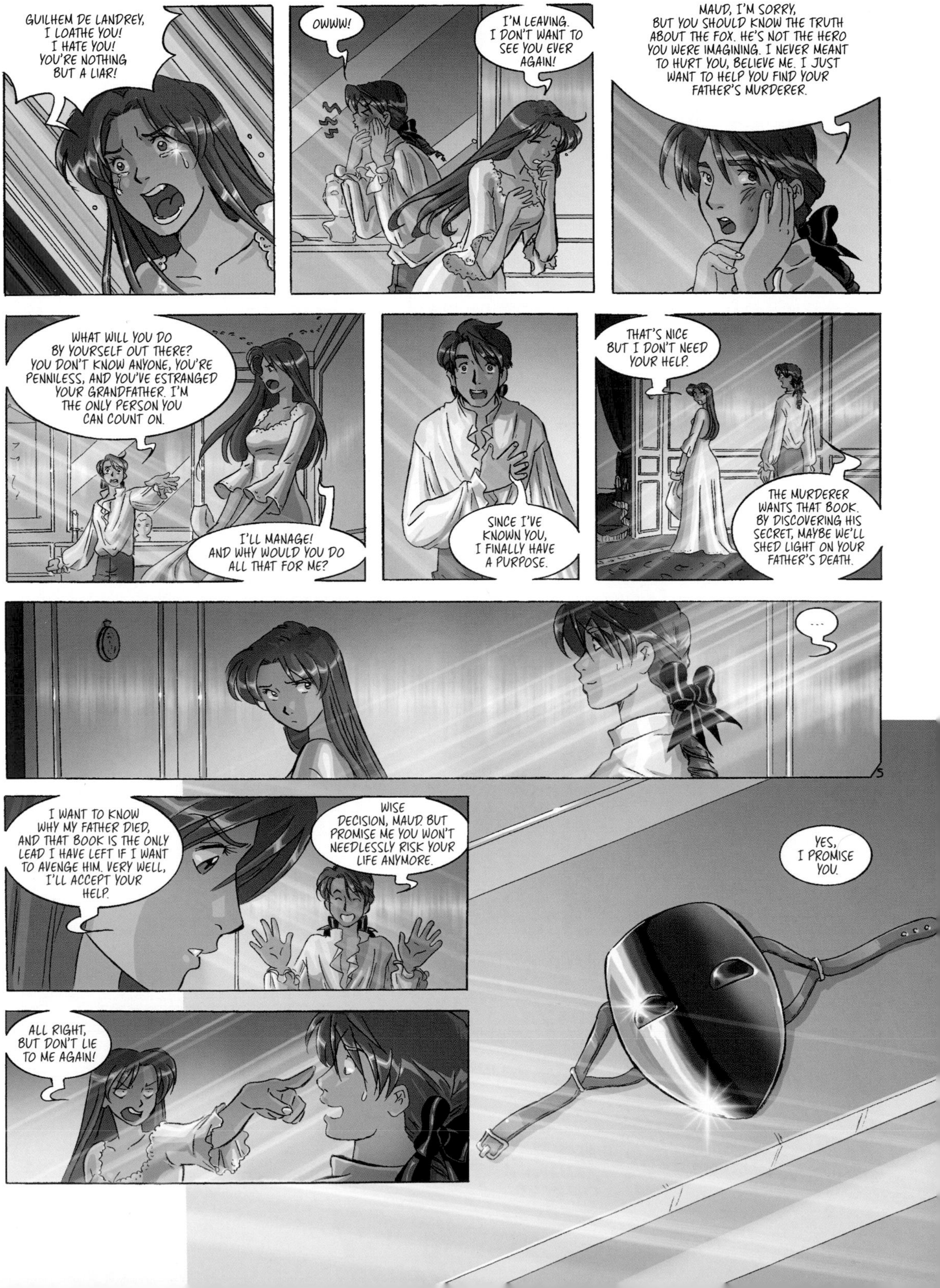
GUILHEM DE LANDREY, I LOATHE YOU! I HATE YOU! YOU'RE NOTHING BUT A LIAR!
OWWW!
I'M LEAVING. I DON'T WANT TO SEE YOU EVER AGAIN!
MAUD, I'M SORRY, BUT YOU SHOULD KNOW THE TRUTH ABOUT THE FOX. HE'S NOT THE HERO YOU WERE IMAGINING. I NEVER MEANT TO HURT YOU, BELIEVE ME. I JUST WANT TO HELP YOU FIND YOUR FATHER'S MURDERER.
WHAT WILL YOU DO BY YOURSELF OUT THERE? YOU DON'T KNOW ANYONE, YOU'RE PENNILESS, AND YOU'VE ESTRANGED YOUR GRANDFATHER. I'M THE ONLY PERSON YOU CAN COUNT ON.
I'LL MANAGE! AND WHY WOULD YOU DO ALL THAT FOR ME?
SINCE I'VE KNOWN YOU, I FINALLY HAVE A PURPOSE.
THAT'S NICE BUT I DON'T NEED YOUR HELP.
THE MURDERER WANTS THAT BOOK. BY DISCOVERING HIS SECRET, MAYBE WE'LL SHED LIGHT ON YOUR FATHER'S DEATH.
...
I WANT TO KNOW WHY MY FATHER DIED, AND THAT BOOK IS THE ONLY LEAD I HAVE LEFT IF I WANT TO AVENGE HIM. VERY WELL, I'LL ACCEPT YOUR HELP.
WISE DECISION, MAUD. BUT PROMISE ME YOU WON'T NEEDLESSLY RISK YOUR LIFE ANYMORE.
YES, I PROMISE YOU.
ALL RIGHT, BUT DON'T LIE TO ME AGAIN!

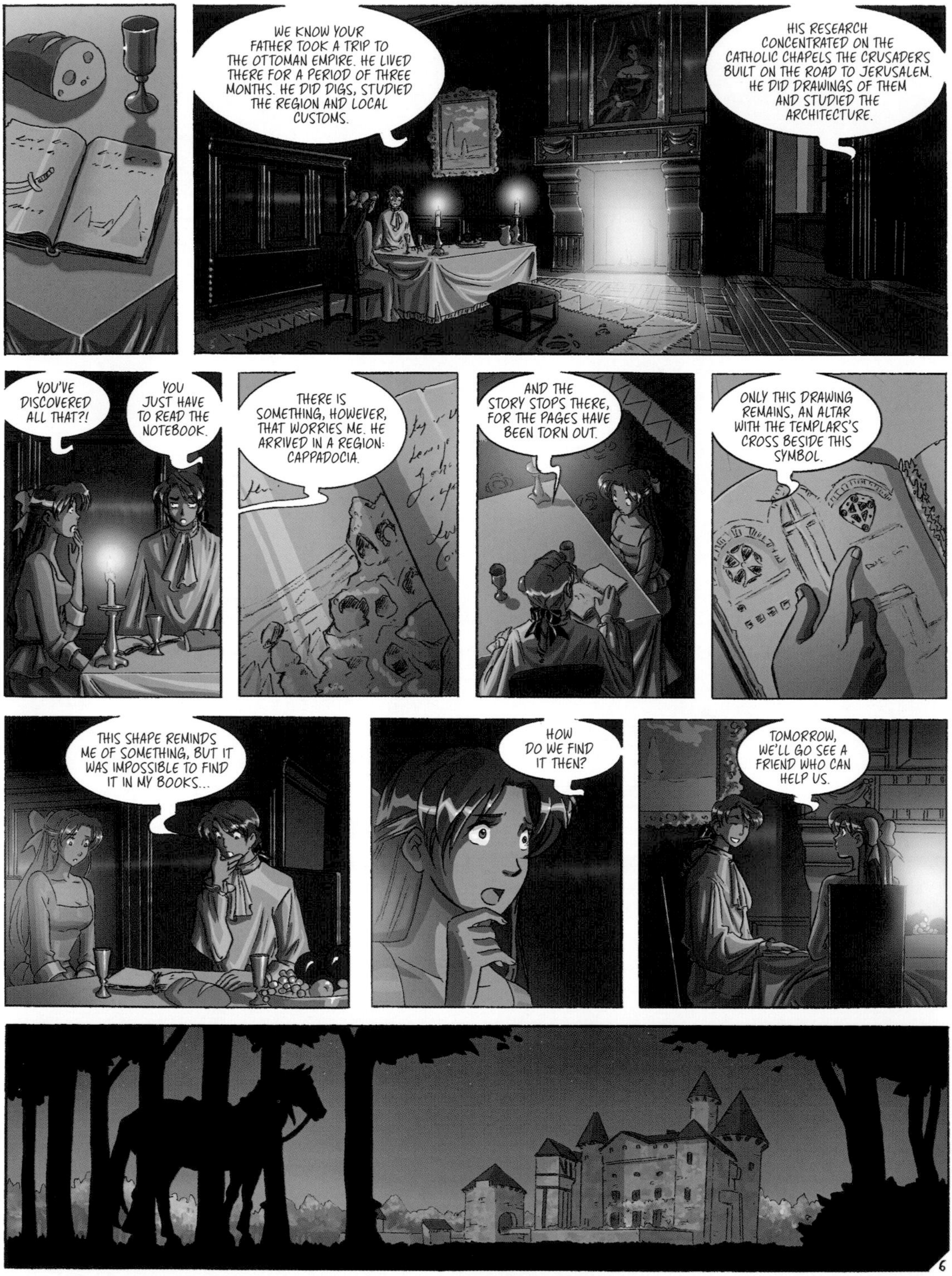
WE KNOW YOUR FATHER TOOK A TRIP TO THE OTTOMAN EMPIRE. HE LIVED THERE FOR A PERIOD OF THREE MONTHS. HE DID DIGS, STUDIED THE REGION AND LOCAL CUSTOMS.
HIS RESEARCH CONCENTRATED ON THE CATHOLIC CHAPELS THE CRUSADERS BUILT ON THE ROAD TO JERUSALEM. HE DID DRAWINGS OF THEM AND STUDIED THE ARCHITECTURE.
YOU'VE DISCOVERED ALL THAT?!
YOU JUST HAVE TO READ THE NOTEBOOK.
THERE IS SOMETHING, HOWEVER, THAT WORRIES ME. HE ARRIVED IN A REGION: CAPPADOCIA.
AND THE STORY STOPS THERE, FOR THE PAGES HAVE BEEN TORN OUT.
ONLY THIS DRAWING REMAINS, AN ALTAR WITH THE TEMPLARS'S CROSS BESIDE THIS SYMBOL.
THIS SHAPE REMINDS ME OF SOMETHING, BUT IT WAS IMPOSSIBLE TO FIND IT IN MY BOOKS...
HOW DO WE FIND IT THEN?
TOMORROW, WE'LL GO SEE A FRIEND WHO CAN HELP US.
6

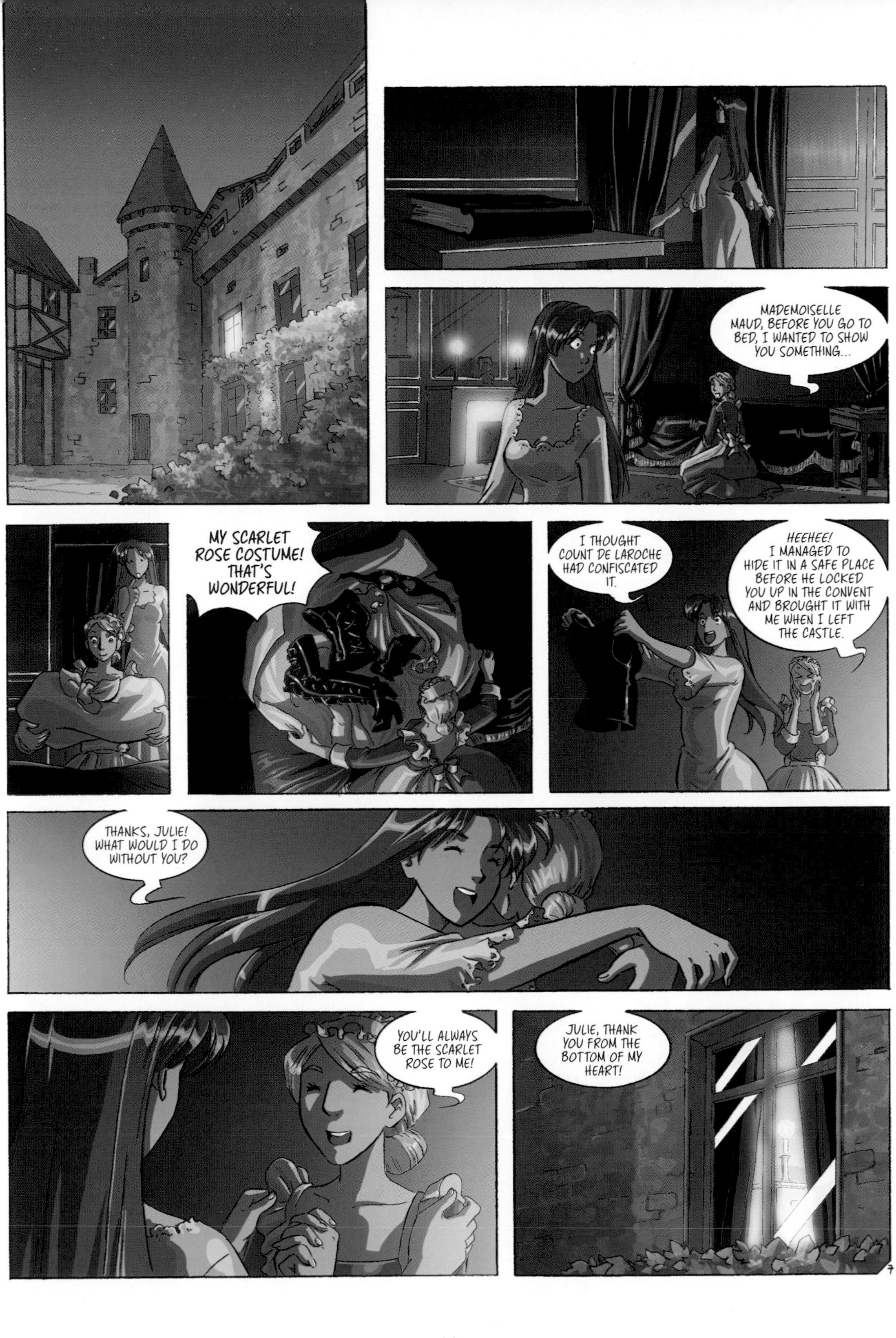
MADEMOISELLE MAUD, BEFORE YOU GO TO BED, I WANTED TO SHOW YOU SOMETHING...
MY SCARLET ROSE COSTUME! THAT'S WONDERFUL!
I THOUGHT COUNT DE LAROCHE HAD CONFISCATED IT.
HEEHEE! I MANAGED TO HIDE IT IN A SAFE PLACE BEFORE HE LOCKED YOU UP IN THE CONVENT AND BROUGHT IT WITH ME WHEN I LEFT THE CASTLE.
THANKS, JULIE! WHAT WOULD I DO WITHOUT YOU?
YOU'LL ALWAYS BE THE SCARLET ROSE TO ME!
JULIE, THANK YOU FROM THE BOTTOM OF MY HEART!

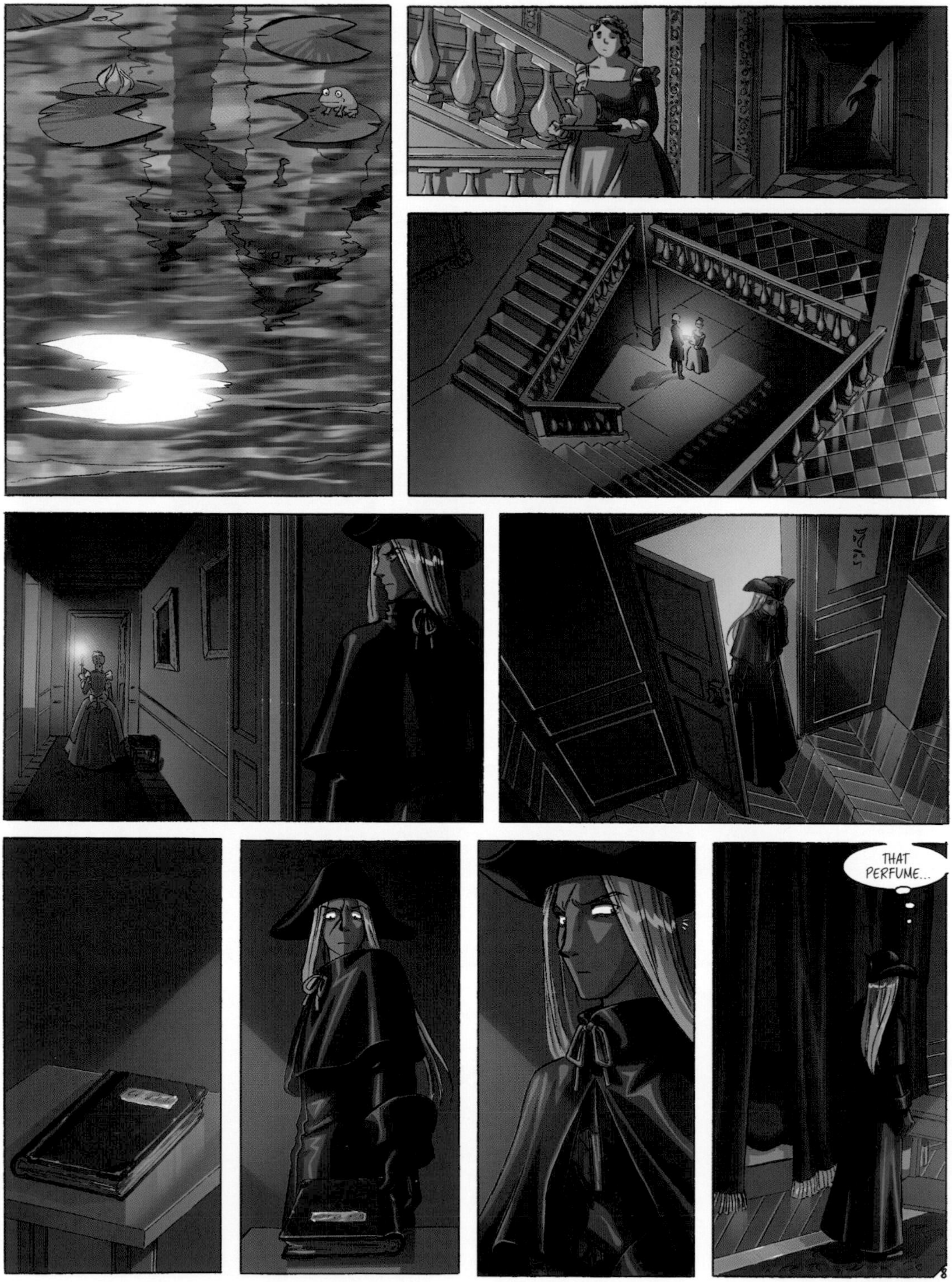
THAT PERFUME...

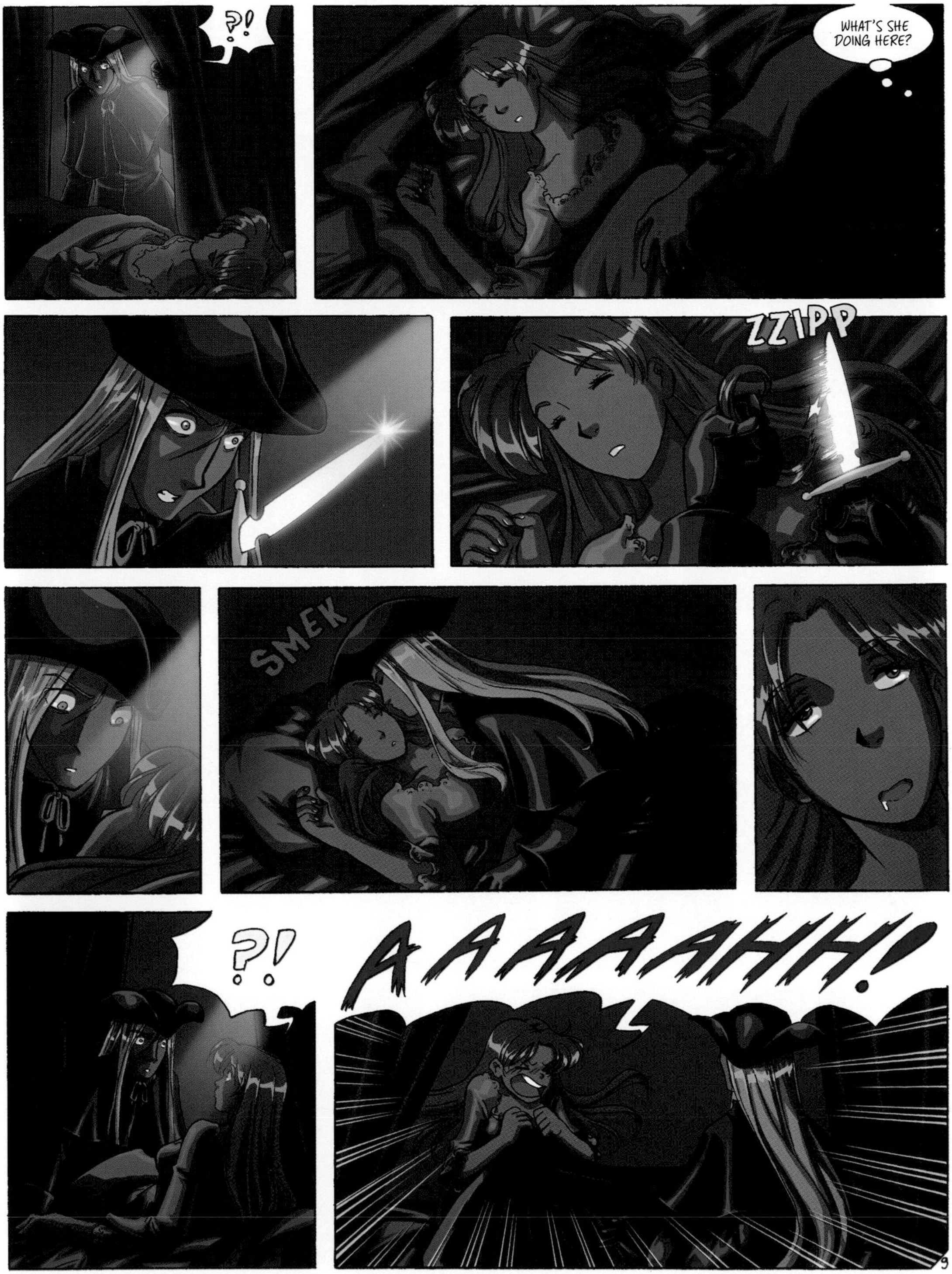
?!
WHAT'S SHE DOING HERE?
ZZIPP
SMEK
?!
AAAAAHH!

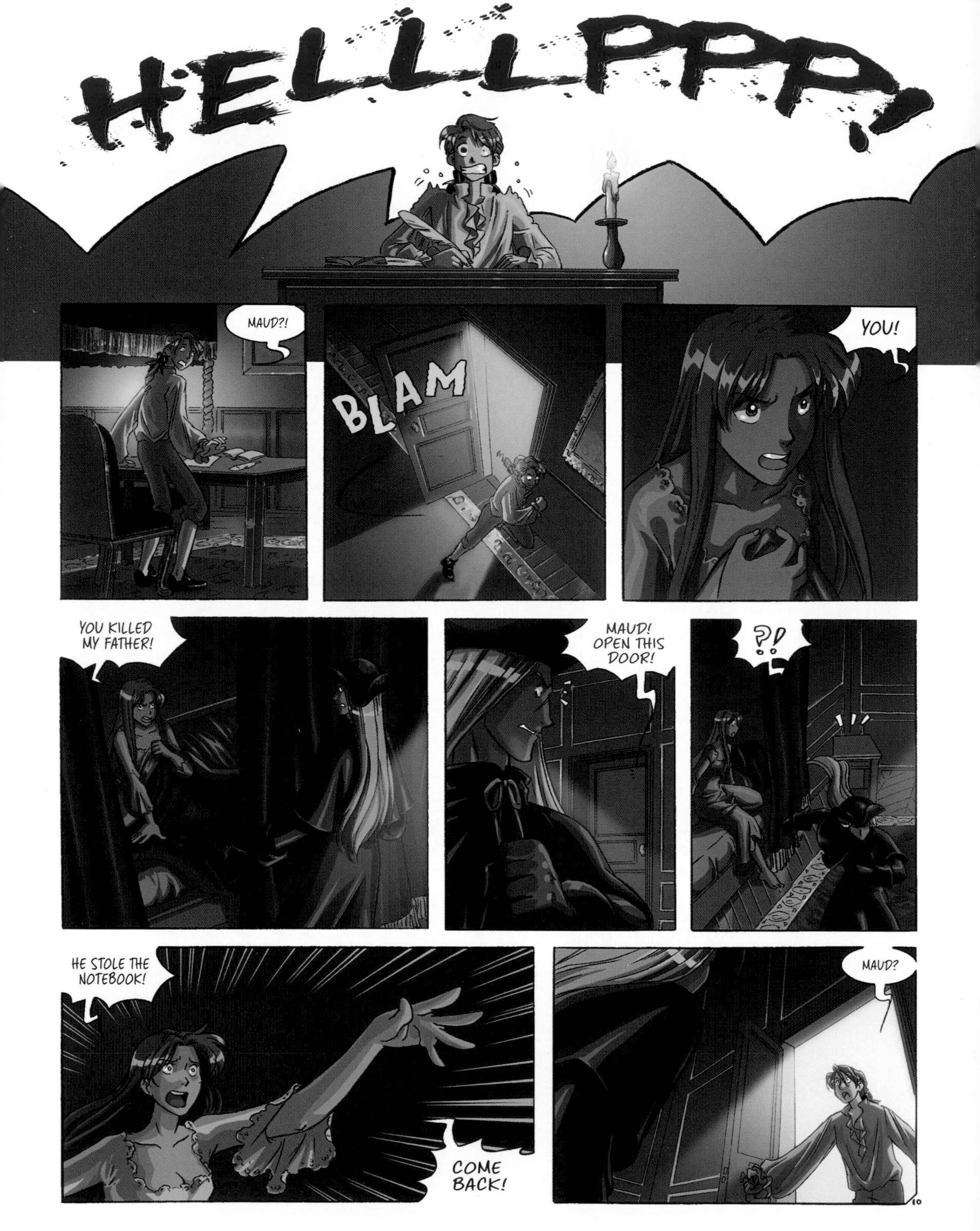
HELLLPPP!
MAUD?!
BLAM
YOU!
YOU KILLED MY FATHER!
MAUD! OPEN THIS DOOR!
?!
HE STOLE THE NOTEBOOK!
COME BACK!
MAUD?
10

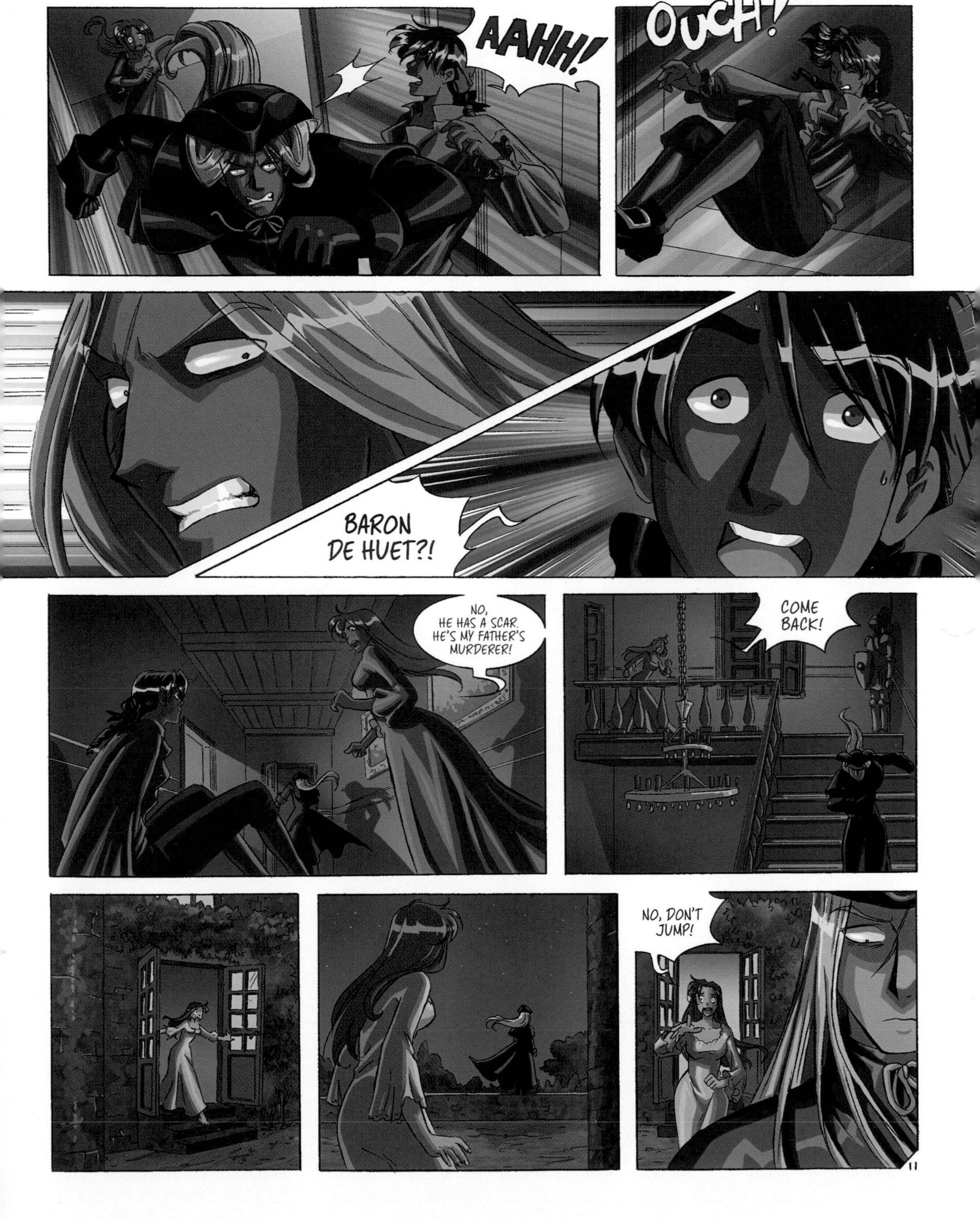
AAHH!
OUCH!
BARON DE HUET?!
NO, HE HAS A SCAR. HE'S MY FATHER'S MURDERER!
COME BACK!
NO, DON'T JUMP!
11

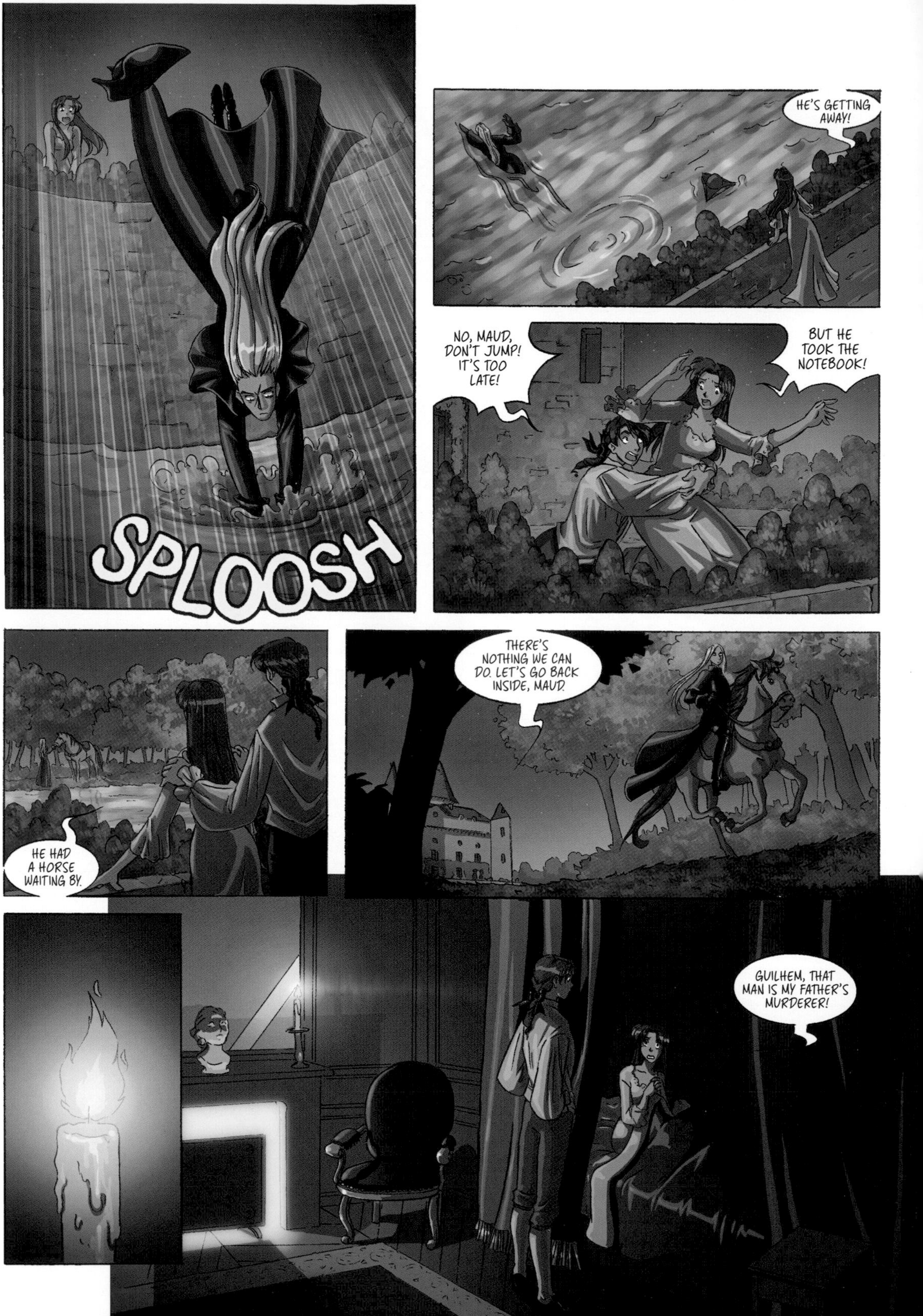
SPLOOSH
HE'S GETTING AWAY!
NO, MAUD, DON'T JUMP! IT'S TOO LATE!
BUT HE TOOK THE NOTEBOOK!
HE HAD A HORSE WAITING BY.
THERE'S NOTHING WE CAN DO. LET'S GO BACK INSIDE, MAUD.
GUILHEM, THAT MAN IS MY FATHER'S MURDERER!

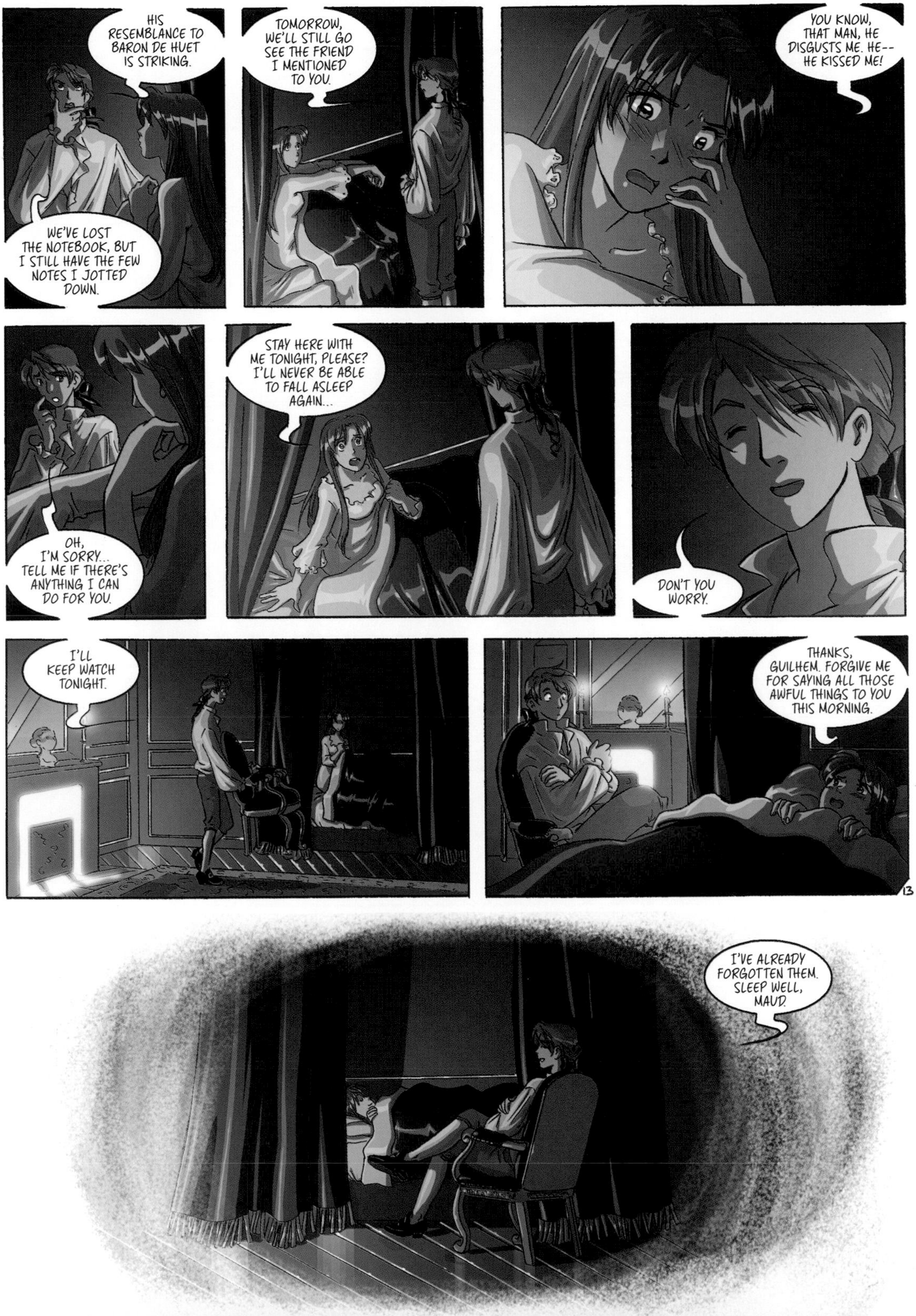
HIS RESEMBLANCE TO BARON DE HUET IS STRIKING.
WE'VE LOST THE NOTEBOOK, BUT I STILL HAVE THE FEW NOTES I JOTTED DOWN.
TOMORROW, WE'LL STILL GO SEE THE FRIEND I MENTIONED TO YOU.
YOU KNOW, THAT MAN, HE DISGUSTS ME. HE-- HE KISSED ME!
OH, I'M SORRY... TELL ME IF THERE'S ANYTHING I CAN DO FOR YOU.
STAY HERE WITH ME TONIGHT, PLEASE? I'LL NEVER BE ABLE TO FALL ASLEEP AGAIN...
DON'T YOU WORRY.
I'LL KEEP WATCH TONIGHT.
THANKS, GUILHEM. FORGIVE ME FOR SAYING ALL THOSE AWFUL THINGS TO YOU THIS MORNING.
13
I'VE ALREADY FORGOTTEN THEM. SLEEP WELL, MAUD.

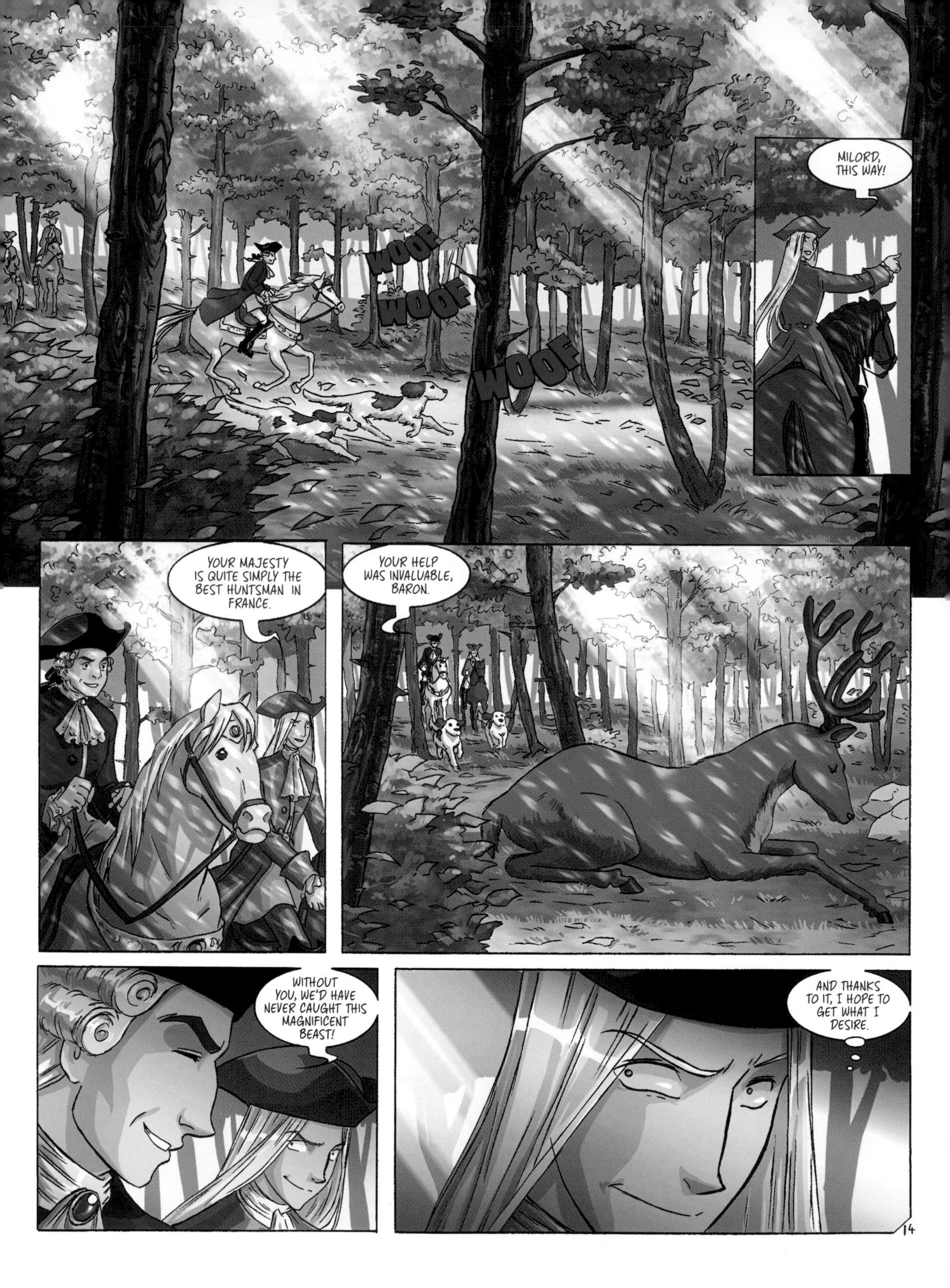
WOOF
WOOF
WOOF
MILORD, THIS WAY!
YOUR MAJESTY IS QUITE SIMPLY THE BEST HUNTSMAN IN FRANCE.
YOUR HELP WAS INVALUABLE, BARON.
WITHOUT YOU, WE'D HAVE NEVER CAUGHT THIS MAGNIFICENT BEAST!
AND THANKS TO IT, I HOPE TO GET WHAT I DESIRE.
14

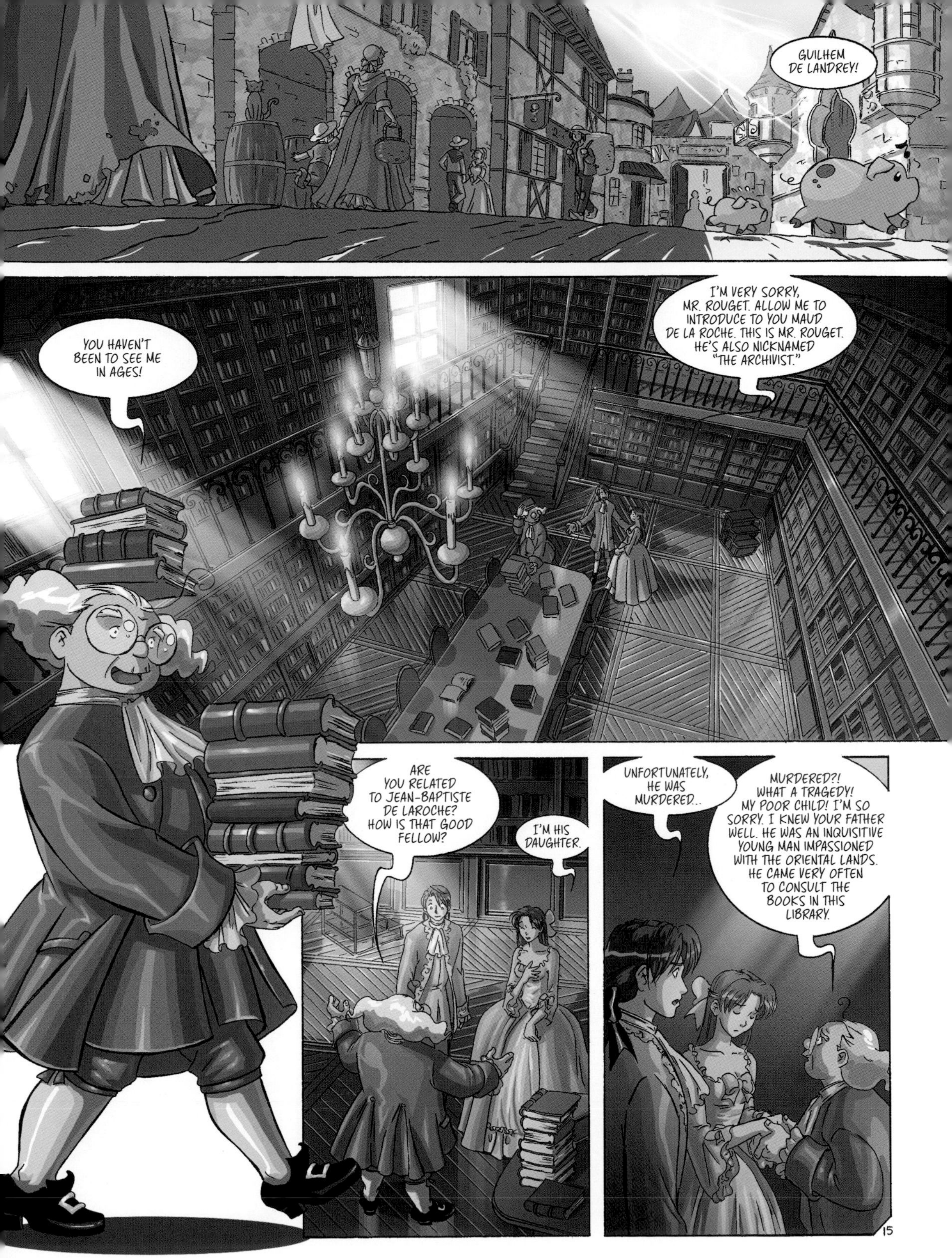
GUILHEM DE LANDREY!
YOU HAVEN'T BEEN TO SEE ME IN AGES!
I'M VERY SORRY, MR. ROUGET. ALLOW ME TO INTRODUCE TO YOU MAUD DE LA ROCHE. THIS IS MR. ROUGET. HE'S ALSO NICKNAMED "THE ARCHIVIST."
ARE YOU RELATED TO JEAN-BAPTISTE DE LAROCHE? HOW IS THAT GOOD FELLOW?
I'M HIS DAUGHTER.
UNFORTUNATELY, HE WAS MURDERED...
MURDERED?! WHAT A TRAGEDY! MY POOR CHILD! I'M SO SORRY. I KNEW YOUR FATHER WELL. HE WAS AN INQUISITIVE YOUNG MAN IMPASSIONED WITH THE ORIENTAL LANDS. HE CAME VERY OFTEN TO CONSULT THE BOOKS IN THIS LIBRARY.
15

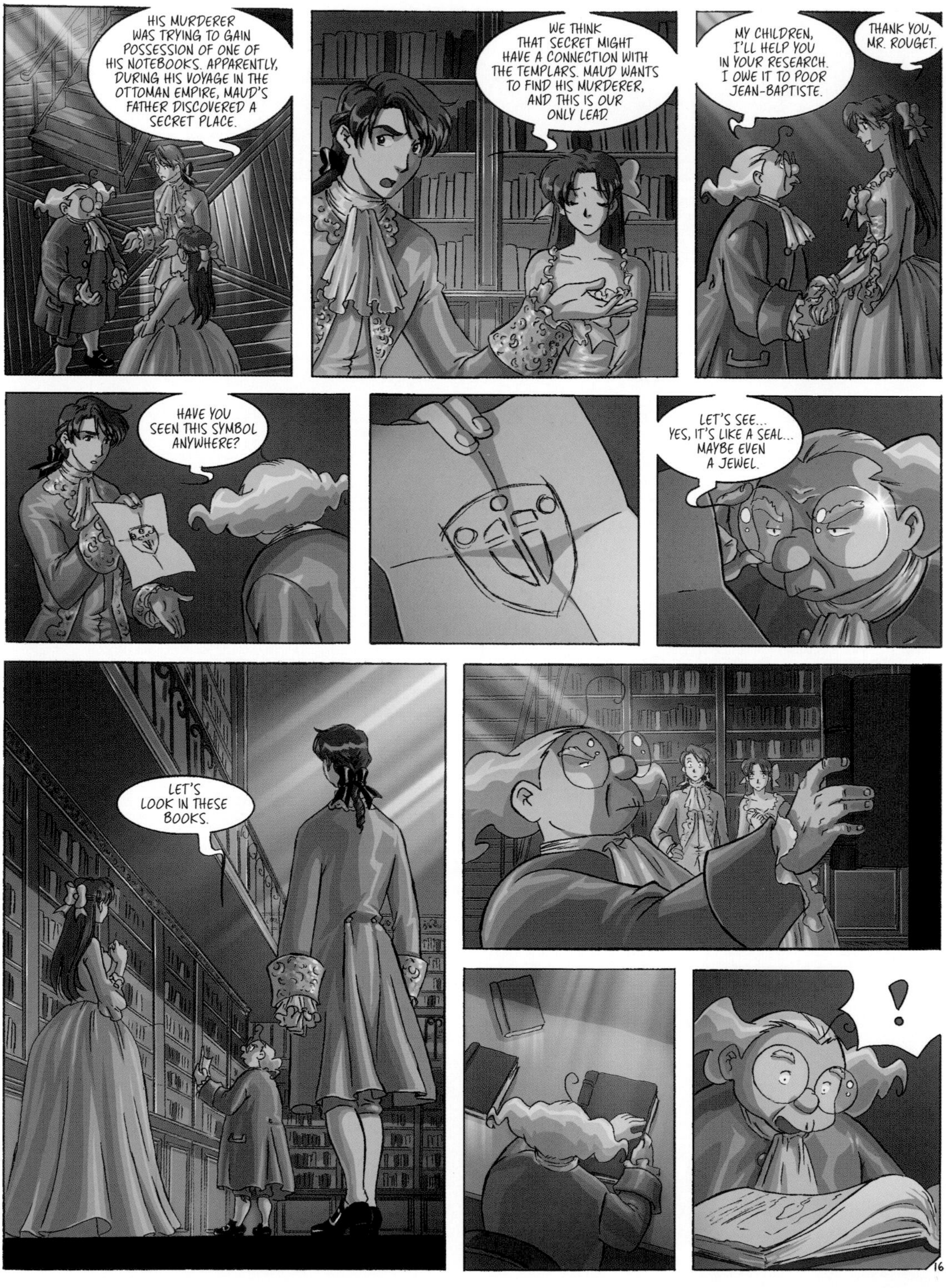
HIS MURDERER WAS TRYING TO GAIN POSSESSION OF ONE OF HIS NOTEBOOKS. APPARENTLY, DURING HIS VOYAGE IN THE OTTOMAN EMPIRE, MAUD'S FATHER DISCOVERED A SECRET PLACE.
WE THINK THAT SECRET MIGHT HAVE A CONNECTION WITH THE TEMPLARS. MAUD WANTS TO FIND HIS MURDERER, AND THIS IS OUR ONLY LEAD.
MY CHILDREN, I'LL HELP YOU IN YOUR RESEARCH. I OWE IT TO POOR JEAN-BAPTISTE.
THANK YOU, MR. ROUGET.
HAVE YOU SEEN THIS SYMBOL ANYWHERE?
LET'S SEE... YES, IT'S LIKE A SEAL... MAYBE EVEN A JEWEL.
LET'S LOOK IN THESE BOOKS.
!
16

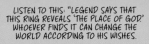

LISTEN TO THIS: "LEGEND SAYS THAT THIS RING REVEALS 'THE PLACE OF GOD.' WHOEVER FINDS IT CAN CHANGE THE WORLD ACCORDING TO HIS WISHES.

"CONSCIOUS OF THE DANGER THIS PLACE REPRESENTED, THE TEMPLARS HAD IT REMOVED FROM ALL KNOWN MAPS. ACCORDING TO THEM, MANKIND WASN'T READY TO ASSUME SUCH POWER.

"THE RING SHOULD HAVE BEEN DESTROYED BUT, DURING THE ARREST OF THE TEMPLARS BY KING PHILLIP THE FAIR, IT WAS STOLEN FROM ITS OWNER, THE KNIGHT DE HUET, WHO WAS ALSO CALLED THE 'GUARDIAN OF THE SANCTUARY,' BUT NOW, THE RING IS IN THE ROYAL COFFERS."

17

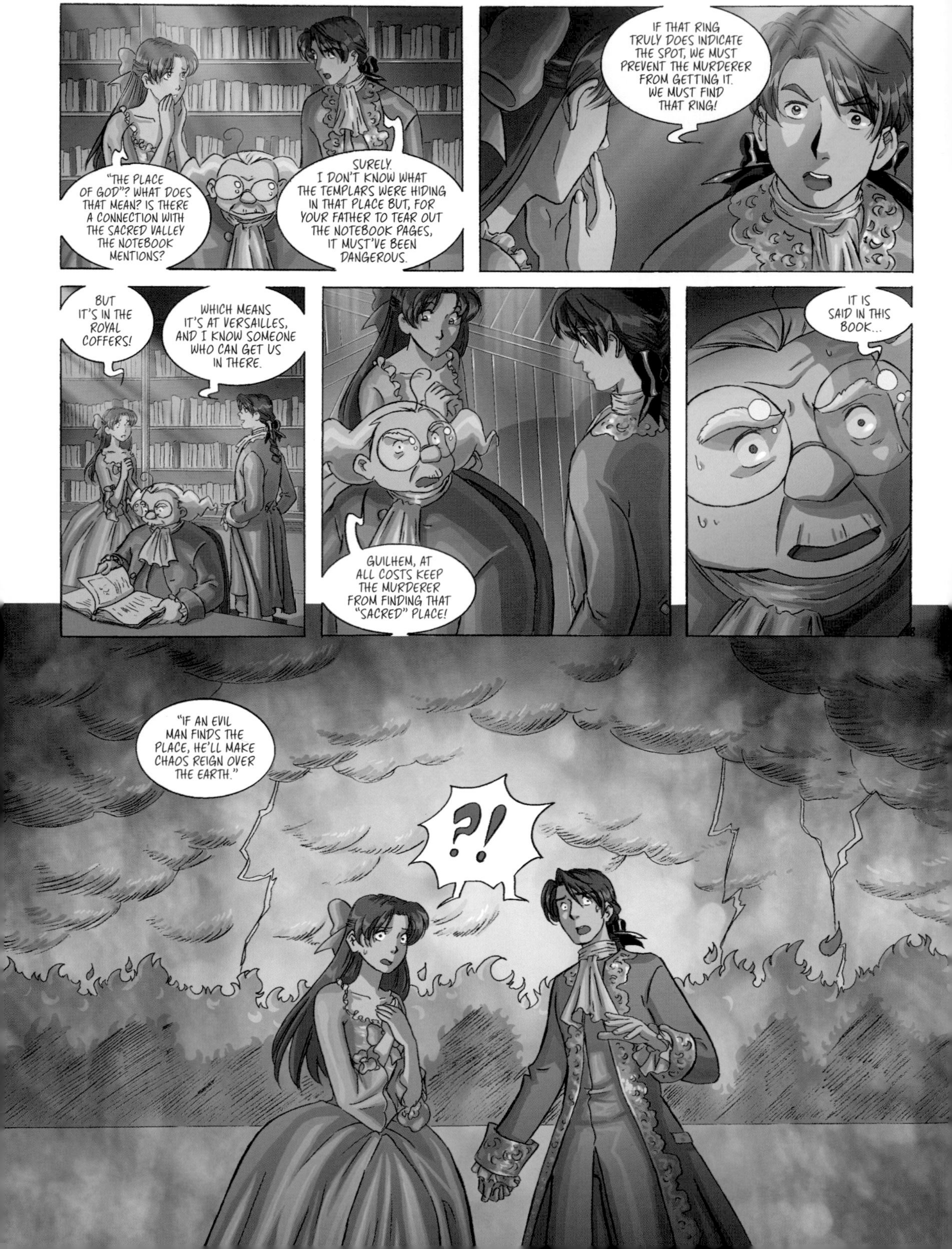
"THE PLACE OF GOD"? WHAT DOES THAT MEAN? IS THERE A CONNECTION WITH THE SACRED VALLEY THE NOTEBOOK MENTIONS?
SURELY. I DON'T KNOW WHAT THE TEMPLARS WERE HIDING IN THAT PLACE BUT, FOR YOUR FATHER TO TEAR OUT THE NOTEBOOK PAGES, IT MUST'VE BEEN DANGEROUS.
IF THAT RING TRULY DOES INDICATE THE SPOT, WE MUST PREVENT THE MURDERER FROM GETTING IT. WE MUST FIND THAT RING!
BUT IT'S IN THE ROYAL COFFERS!
WHICH MEANS IT'S AT VERSAILLES, AND I KNOW SOMEONE WHO CAN GET US IN THERE.
GUILHEM, AT ALL COSTS KEEP THE MURDERER FROM FINDING THAT "SACRED" PLACE!
IT IS SAID IN THIS BOOK...
"IF AN EVIL MAN FINDS THE PLACE, HE'LL MAKE CHAOS REIGN OVER THE EARTH."
?!

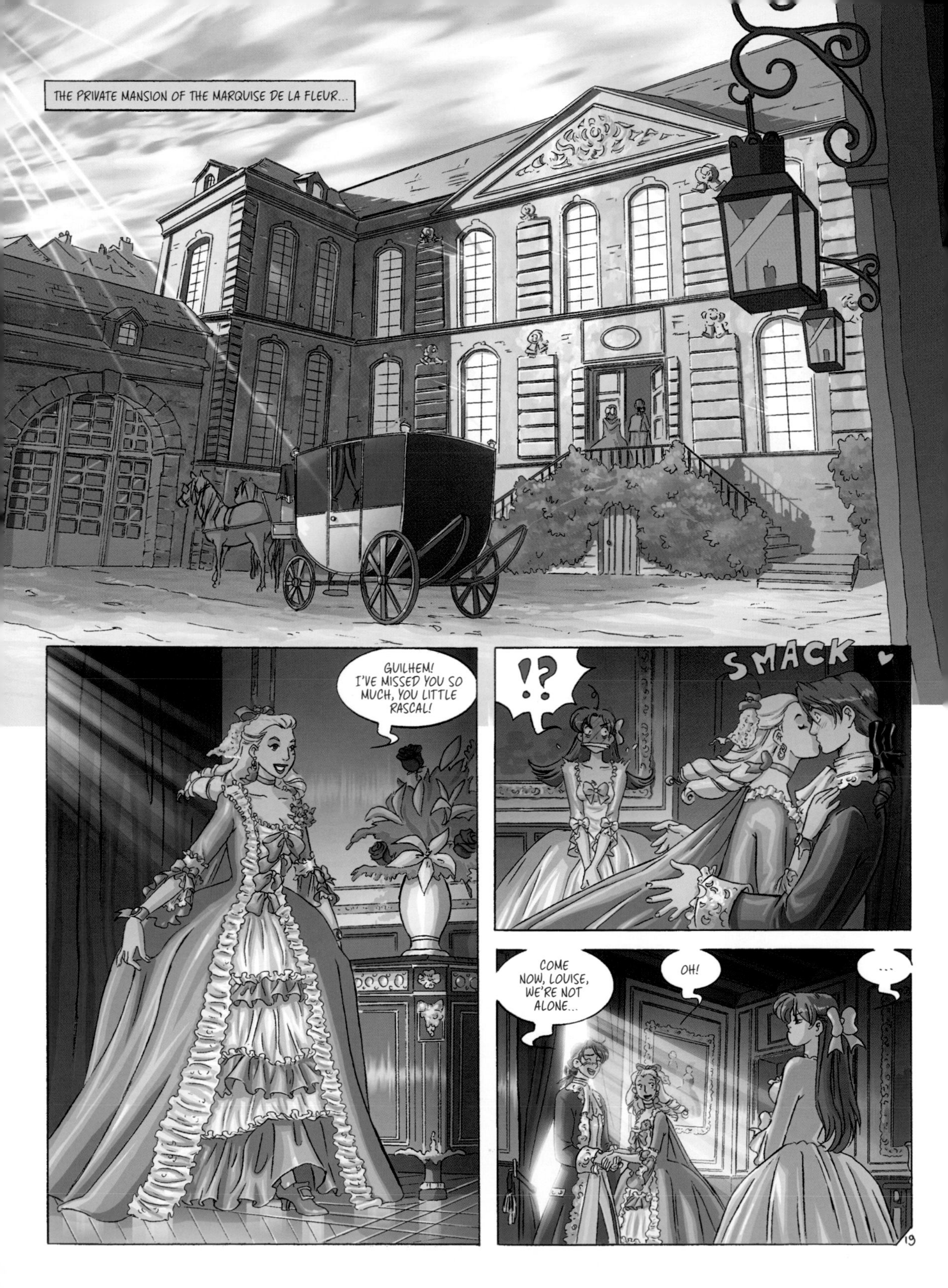
THE PRIVATE MANSION OF THE MARQUISE DE LA FLEUR...
GUILHEM! I'VE MISSED YOU SO MUCH, YOU LITTLE RASCAL!
!?
SMACK
COME NOW, LOUISE, WE'RE NOT ALONE...
OH!
...
19

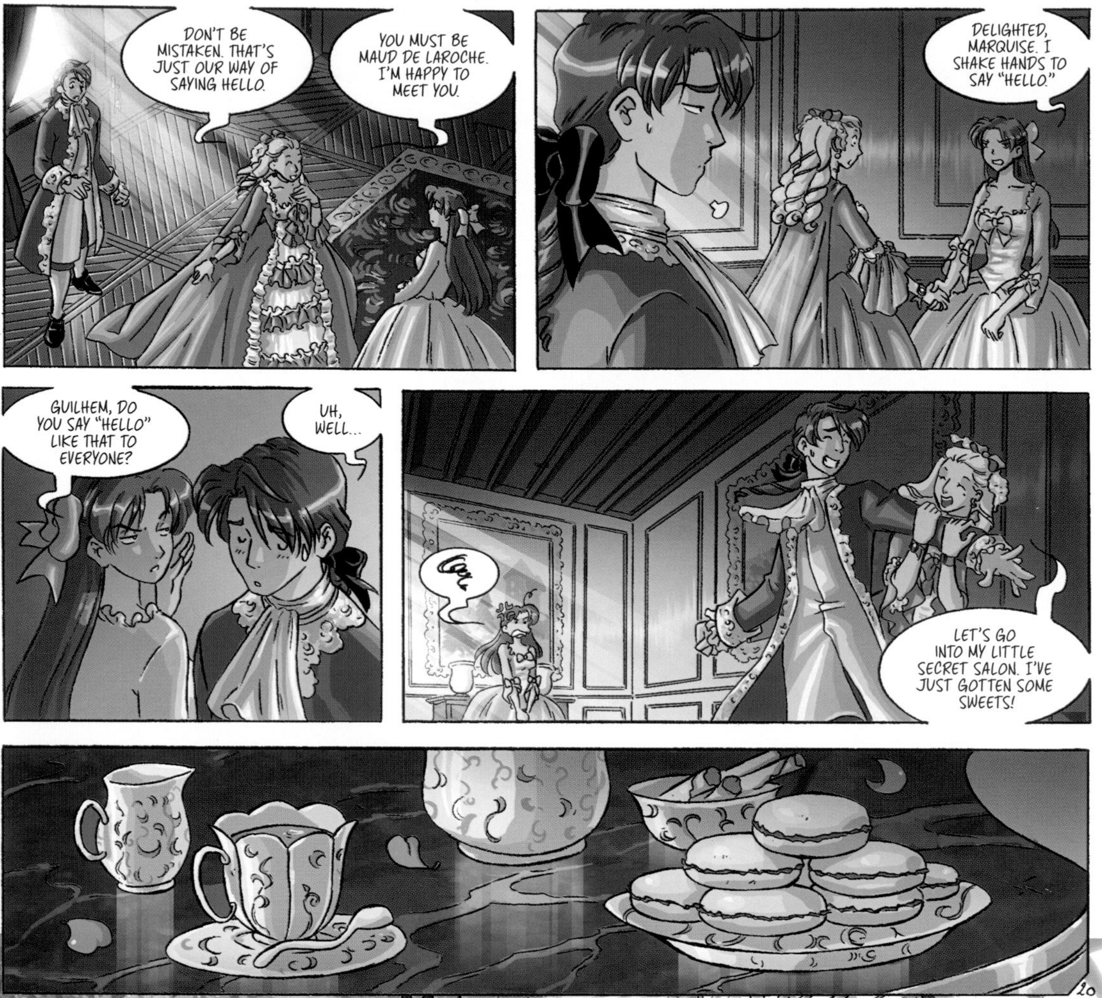
DON'T BE MISTAKEN. THAT'S JUST OUR WAY OF SAYING HELLO.
YOU MUST BE MAUD DE LAROCHE. I'M HAPPY TO MEET YOU.
DELIGHTED, MARQUISE. I SHAKE HANDS TO SAY "HELLO."
GUILHEM, DO YOU SAY "HELLO" LIKE THAT TO EVERYONE?
UH, WELL...
LET'S GO INTO MY LITTLE SECRET SALON. I'VE JUST GOTTEN SOME SWEETS!

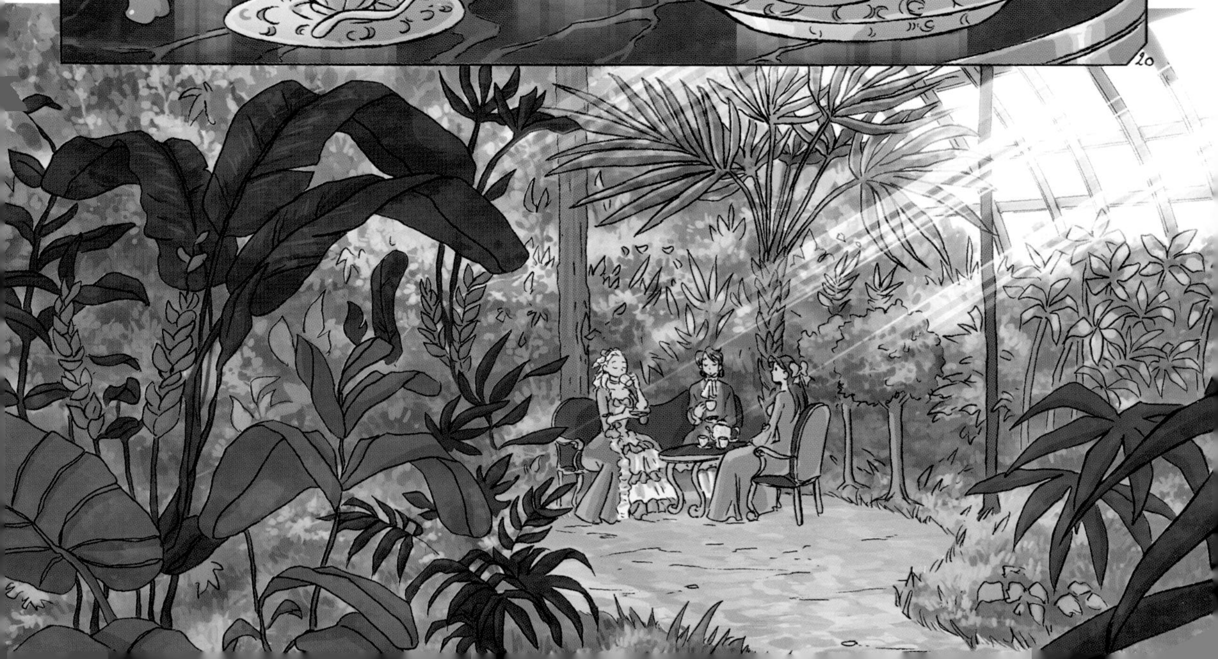

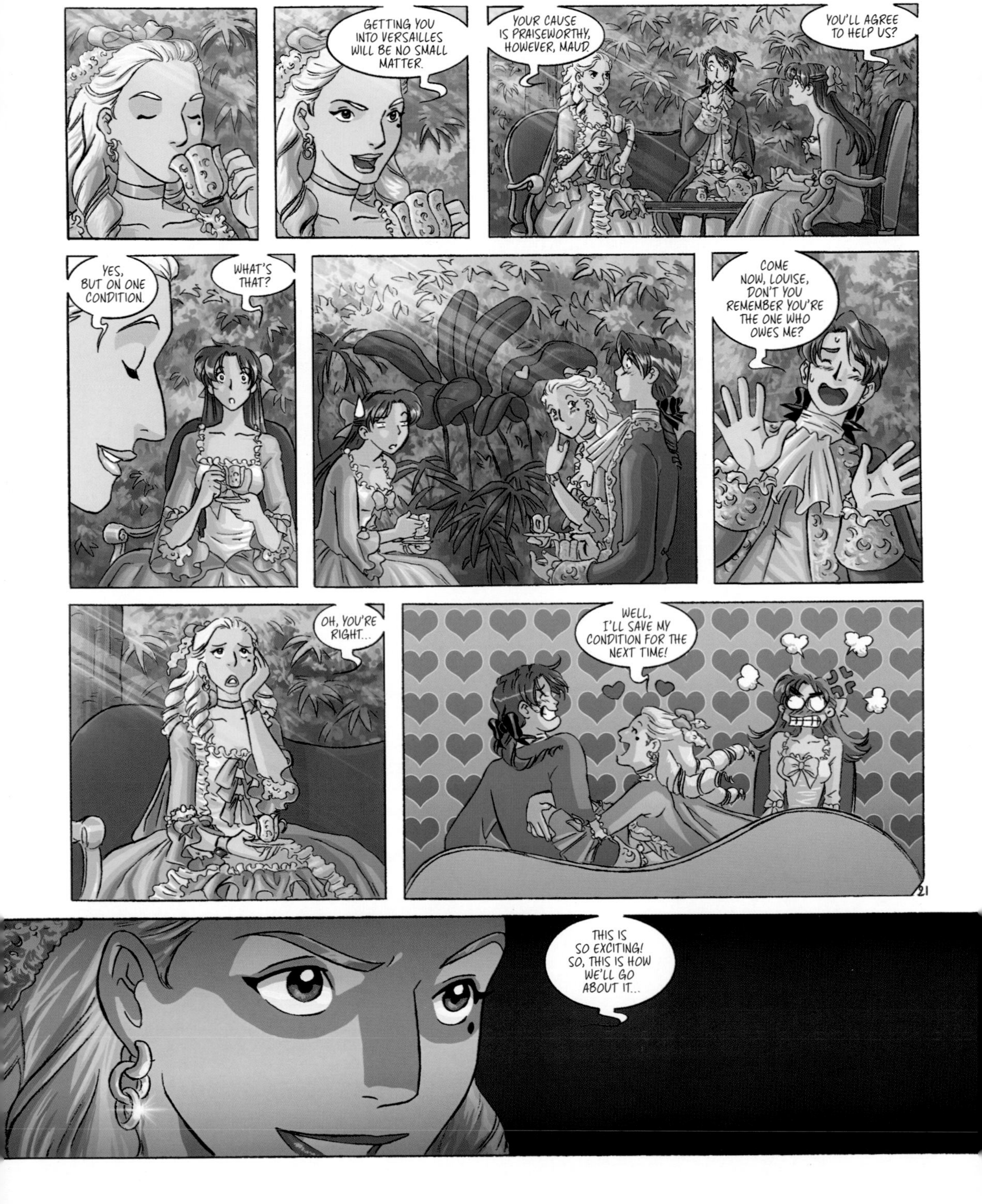
GETTING YOU INTO VERSAILLES WILL BE NO SMALL MATTER.
YOUR CAUSE IS PRAISEWORTHY, HOWEVER, MAUD.
YOU'LL AGREE TO HELP US?
YES, BUT ON ONE CONDITION.
WHAT'S THAT?
COME NOW, LOUISE, DON'T YOU REMEMBER YOU'RE THE ONE WHO OWES ME?
OH, YOU'RE RIGHT...
WELL, I'LL SAVE MY CONDITION FOR THE NEXT TIME!
21
THIS IS SO EXCITING! SO, THIS IS HOW WE'LL GO ABOUT IT...

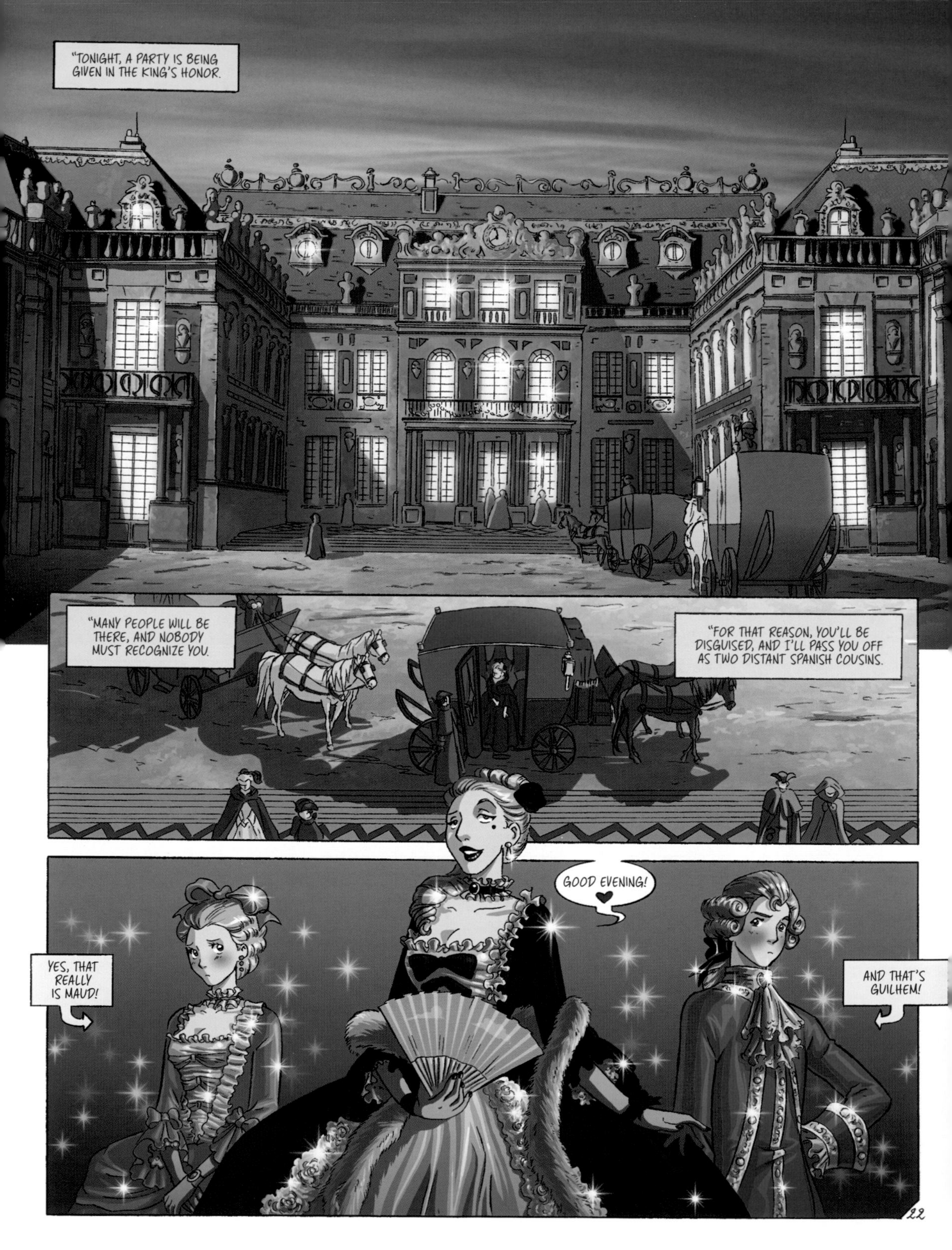
"TONIGHT, A PARTY IS BEING GIVEN IN THE KING'S HONOR.
"MANY PEOPLE WILL BE THERE, AND NOBODY MUST RECOGNIZE YOU.
"FOR THAT REASON, YOU'LL BE DISGUISED, AND I'LL PASS YOU OFF AS TWO DISTANT SPANISH COUSINS.
GOOD EVENING!
YES, THAT REALLY IS MAUD!
AND THAT'S GUILHEM!
22

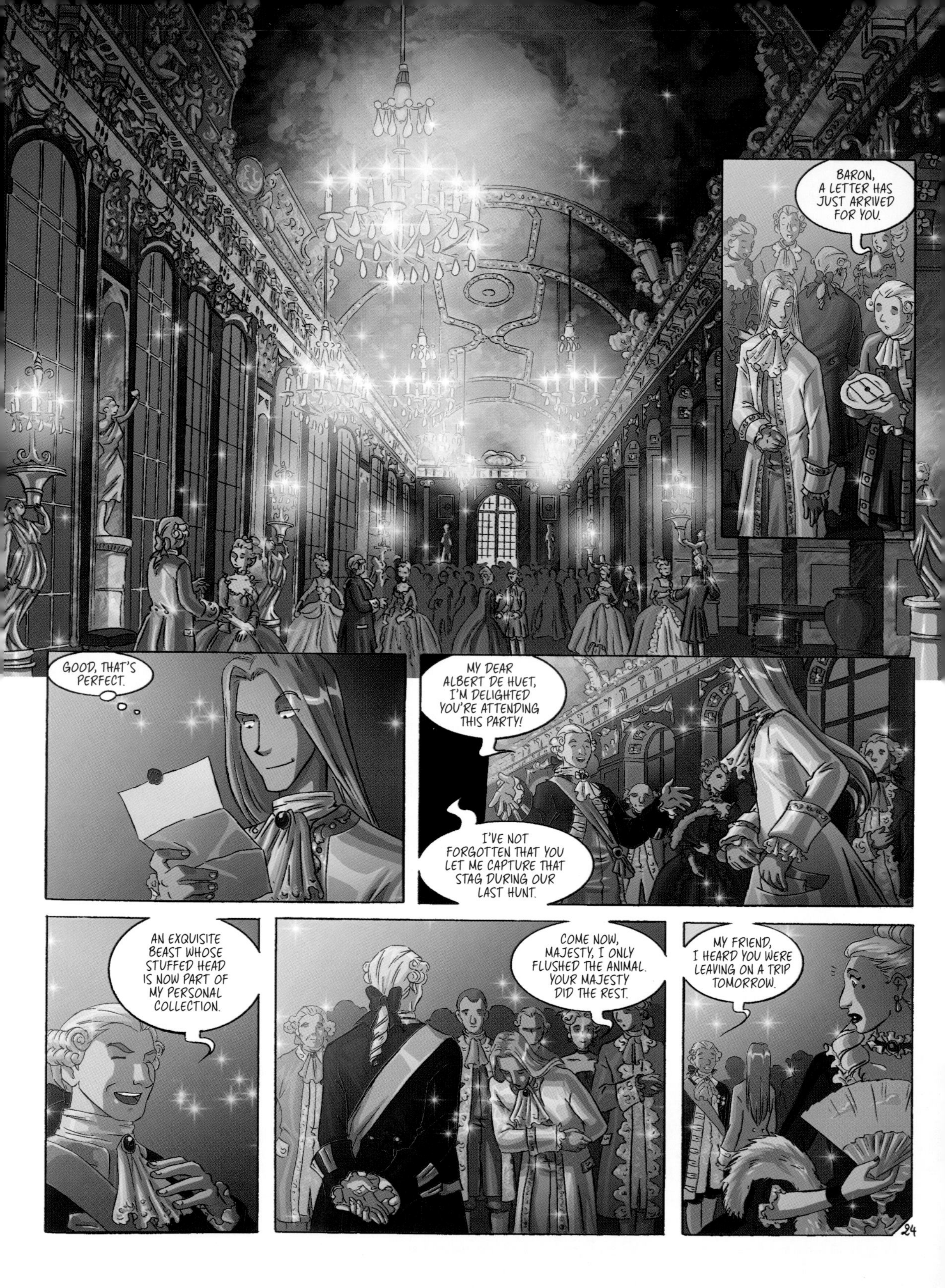
BARON, A LETTER HAS JUST ARRIVED FOR YOU.
GOOD, THAT'S PERFECT.
MY DEAR ALBERT DE HUET, I'M DELIGHTED YOU'RE ATTENDING THIS PARTY!
I'VE NOT FORGOTTEN THAT YOU LET ME CAPTURE THAT STAG DURING OUR LAST HUNT.
AN EXQUISITE BEAST WHOSE STUFFED HEAD IS NOW PART OF MY PERSONAL COLLECTION.
COME NOW, MAJESTY, I ONLY FLUSHED THE ANIMAL. YOUR MAJESTY DID THE REST.
MY FRIEND, I HEARD YOU WERE LEAVING ON A TRIP TOMORROW.
24

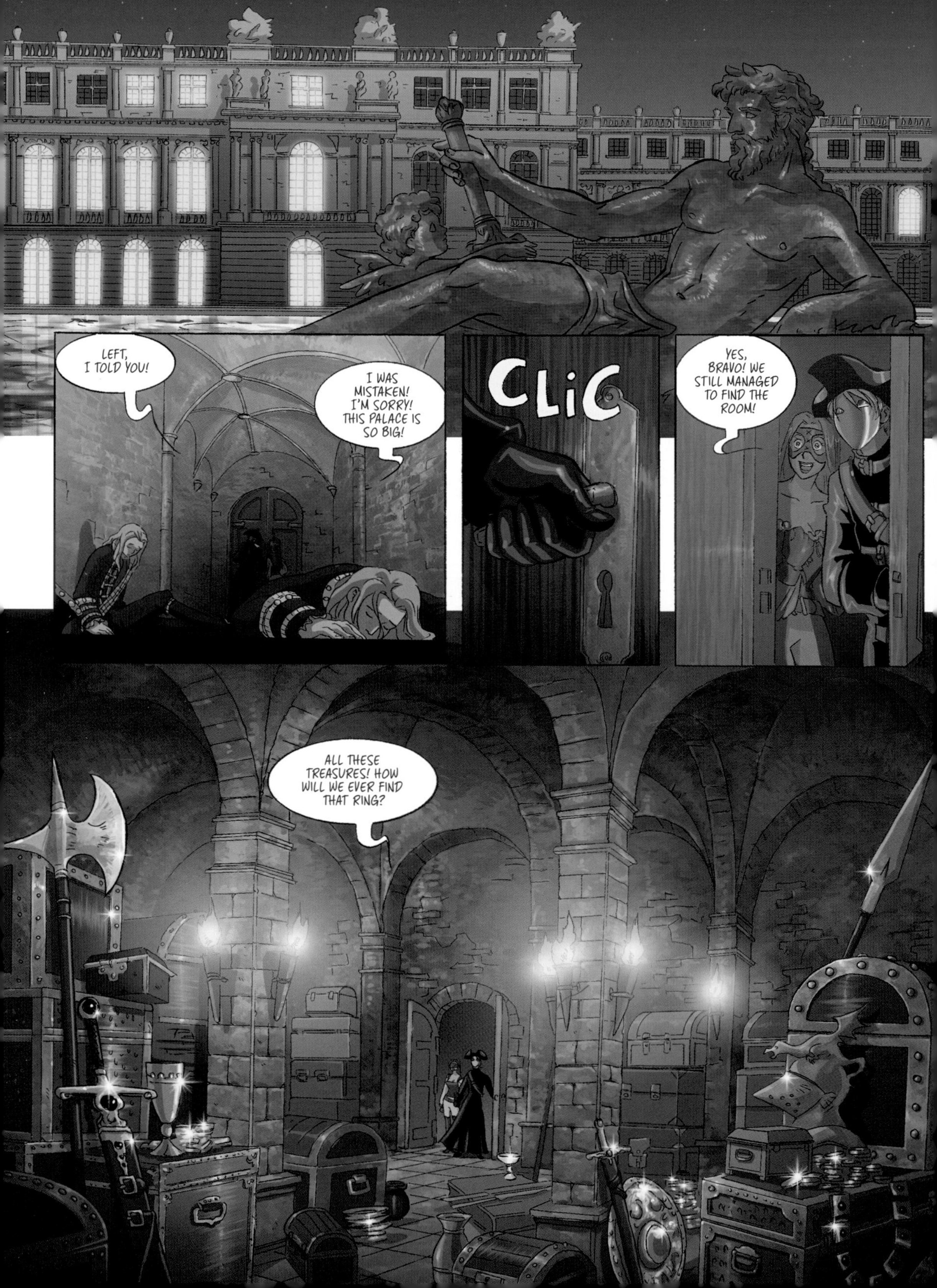
LEFT, I TOLD YOU!
I WAS MISTAKEN! I'M SORRY! THIS PALACE IS SO BIG!
CLIC
YES, BRAVO! WE STILL MANAGED TO FIND THE ROOM!
ALL THESE TREASURES! HOW WILL WE EVER FIND THAT RING?

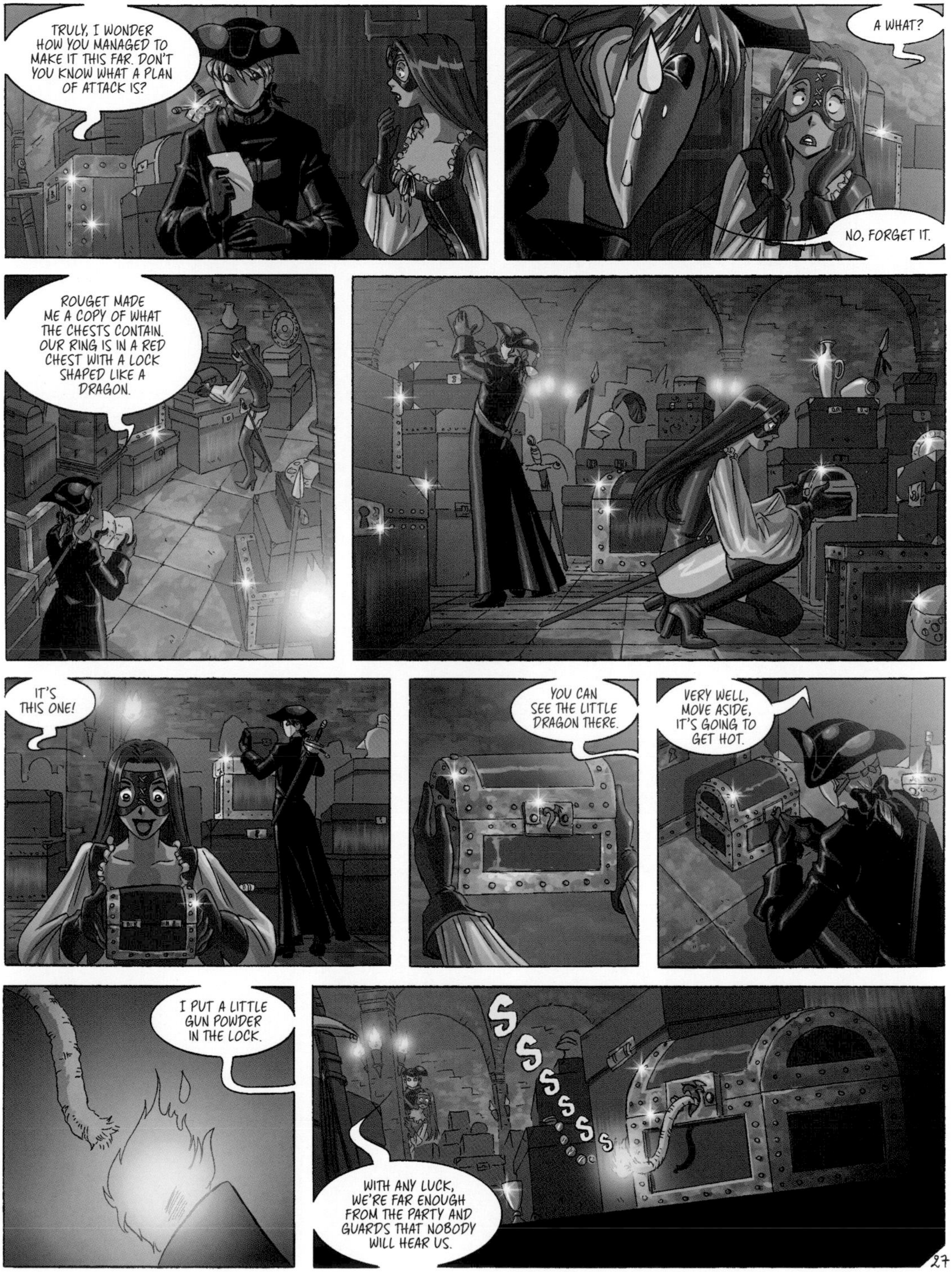
TRULY, I WONDER HOW YOU MANAGED TO MAKE IT THIS FAR. DON'T YOU KNOW WHAT A PLAN OF ATTACK IS?
A WHAT?
NO, FORGET IT.
ROUGET MADE ME A COPY OF WHAT THE CHESTS CONTAIN. OUR RING IS IN A RED CHEST WITH A LOCK SHAPED LIKE A DRAGON.
IT'S THIS ONE!
YOU CAN SEE THE LITTLE DRAGON THERE.
VERY WELL, MOVE ASIDE, IT'S GOING TO GET HOT.
I PUT A LITTLE GUN POWDER IN THE LOCK.
SSSSSSS
WITH ANY LUCK, WE'RE FAR ENOUGH FROM THE PARTY AND GUARDS THAT NOBODY WILL HEAR US.
27

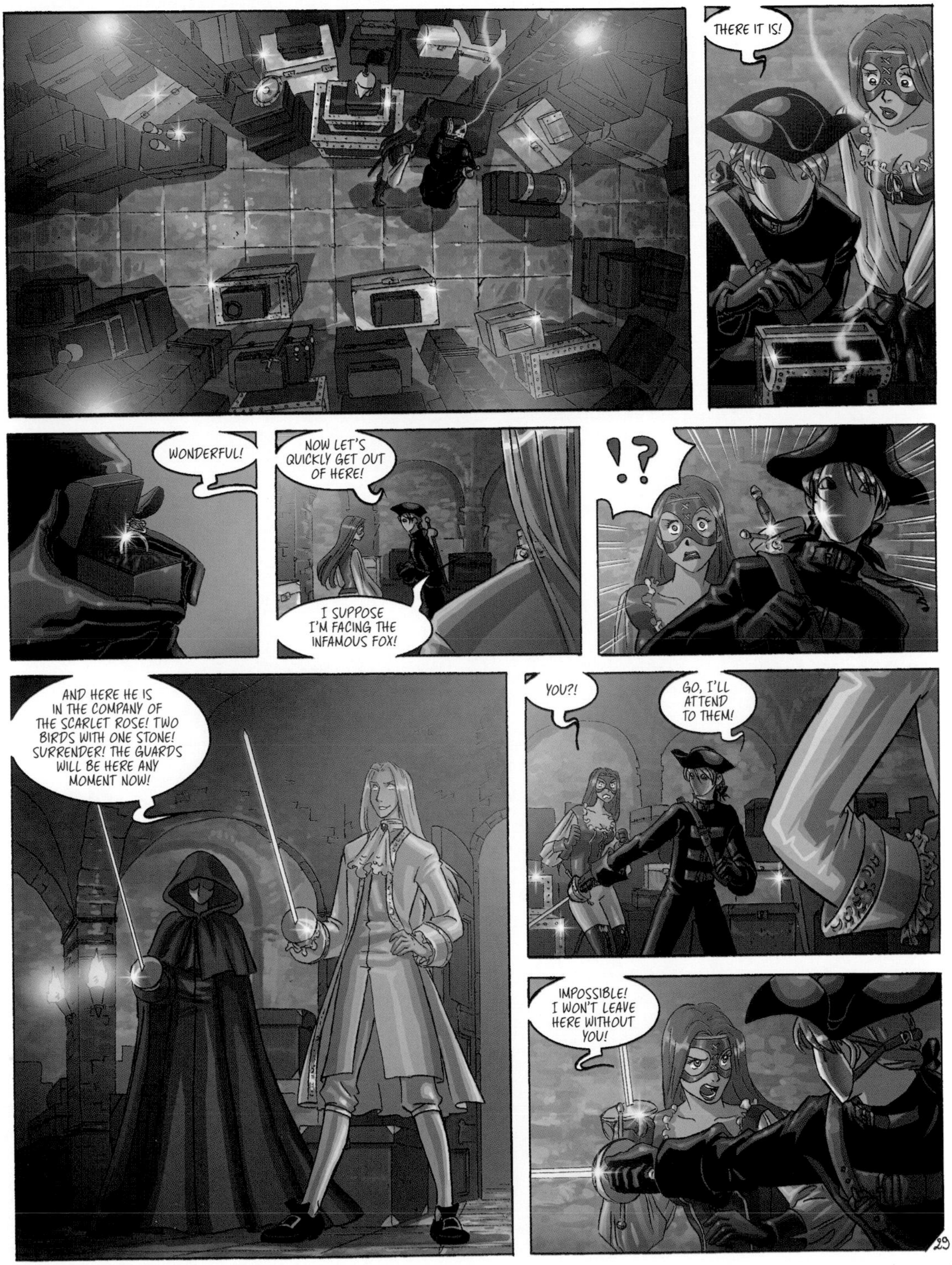
THERE IT IS!
WONDERFUL!
NOW LET'S QUICKLY GET OUT OF HERE!
I SUPPOSE I'M FACING THE INFAMOUS FOX!
!?
AND HERE HE IS IN THE COMPANY OF THE SCARLET ROSE! TWO BIRDS WITH ONE STONE! SURRENDER! THE GUARDS WILL BE HERE ANY MOMENT NOW!
YOU?!
GO, I'LL ATTEND TO THEM!
IMPOSSIBLE! I WON'T LEAVE HERE WITHOUT YOU!
29

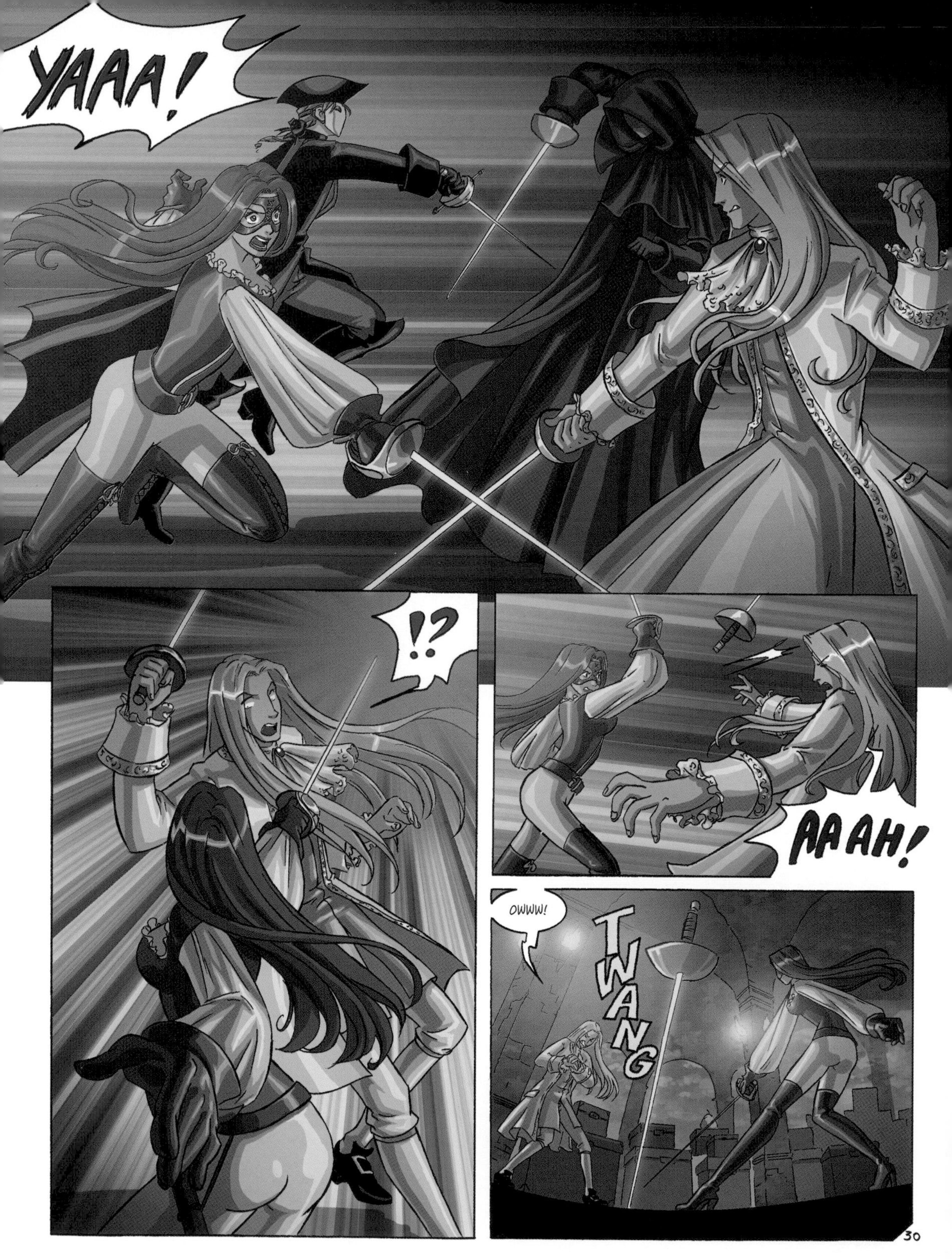
YAAA!
!?
AAAH!
OWWW!
TWANG
30

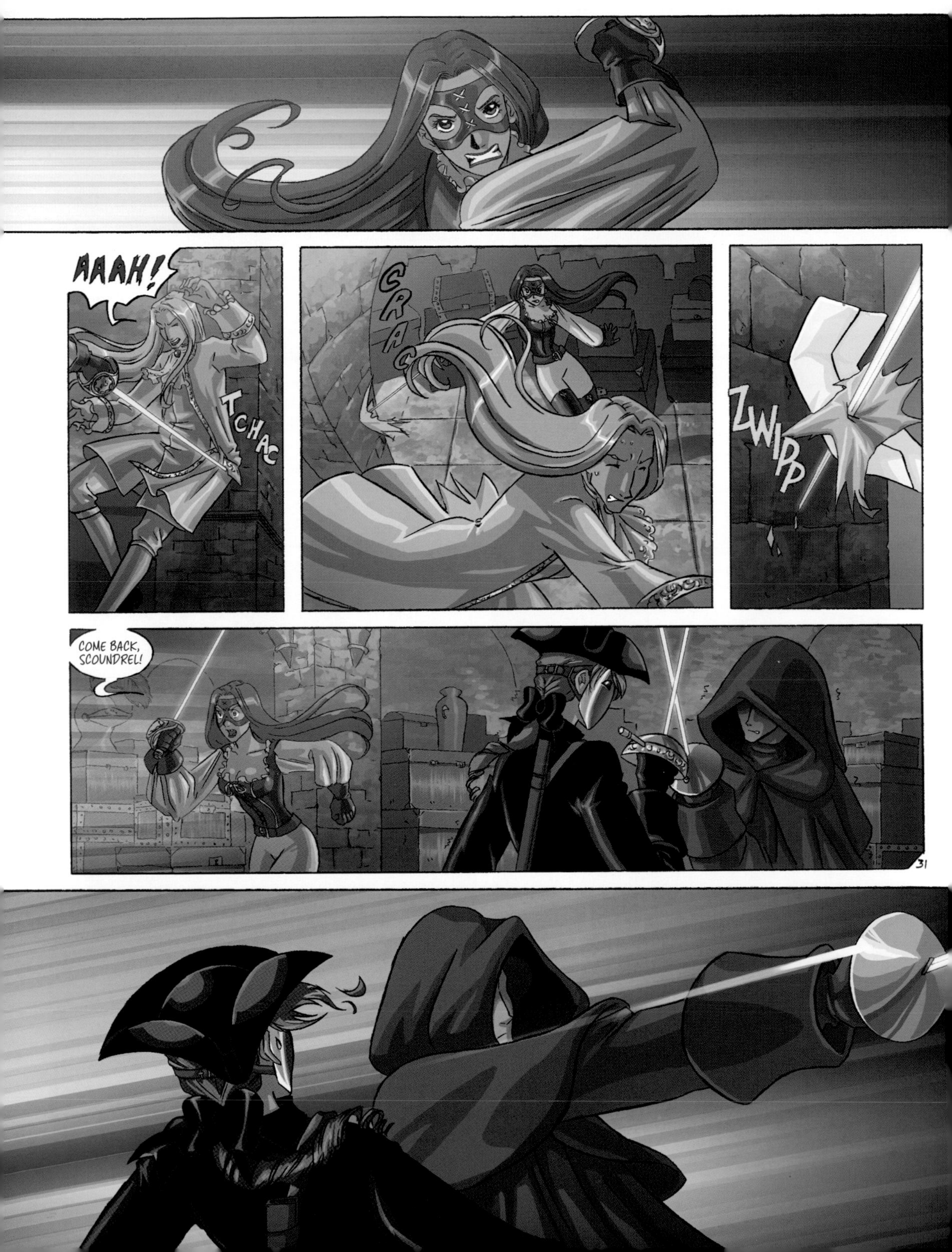

AAAH!
TCHAC
CRAC
ZWIPP
COME BACK, SCOUNDREL!

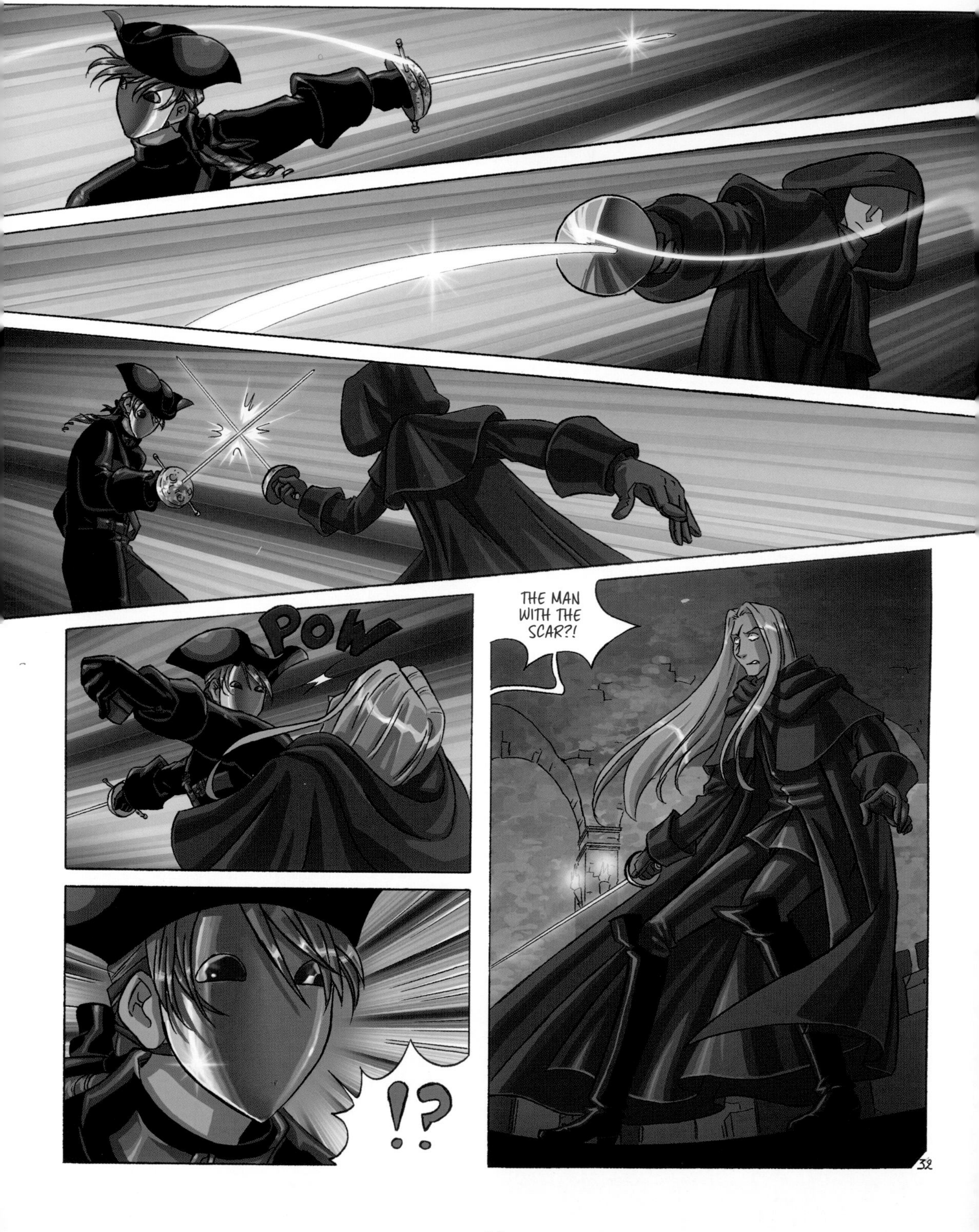
POW
THE MAN WITH THE SCAR?!
!?
32

THERE'S TWO OF YOU?!

OOOF!

AAAH!

ARE YOU--?

IT'S IMPOSSIBLE?!

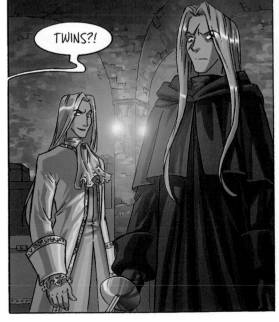

TWINS?!

YES, IT'S ALWAYS A LITTLE SURPRISING, BUT NOW THAT YOU KNOW OUR SECRET...

YOU MUST DIE!

33

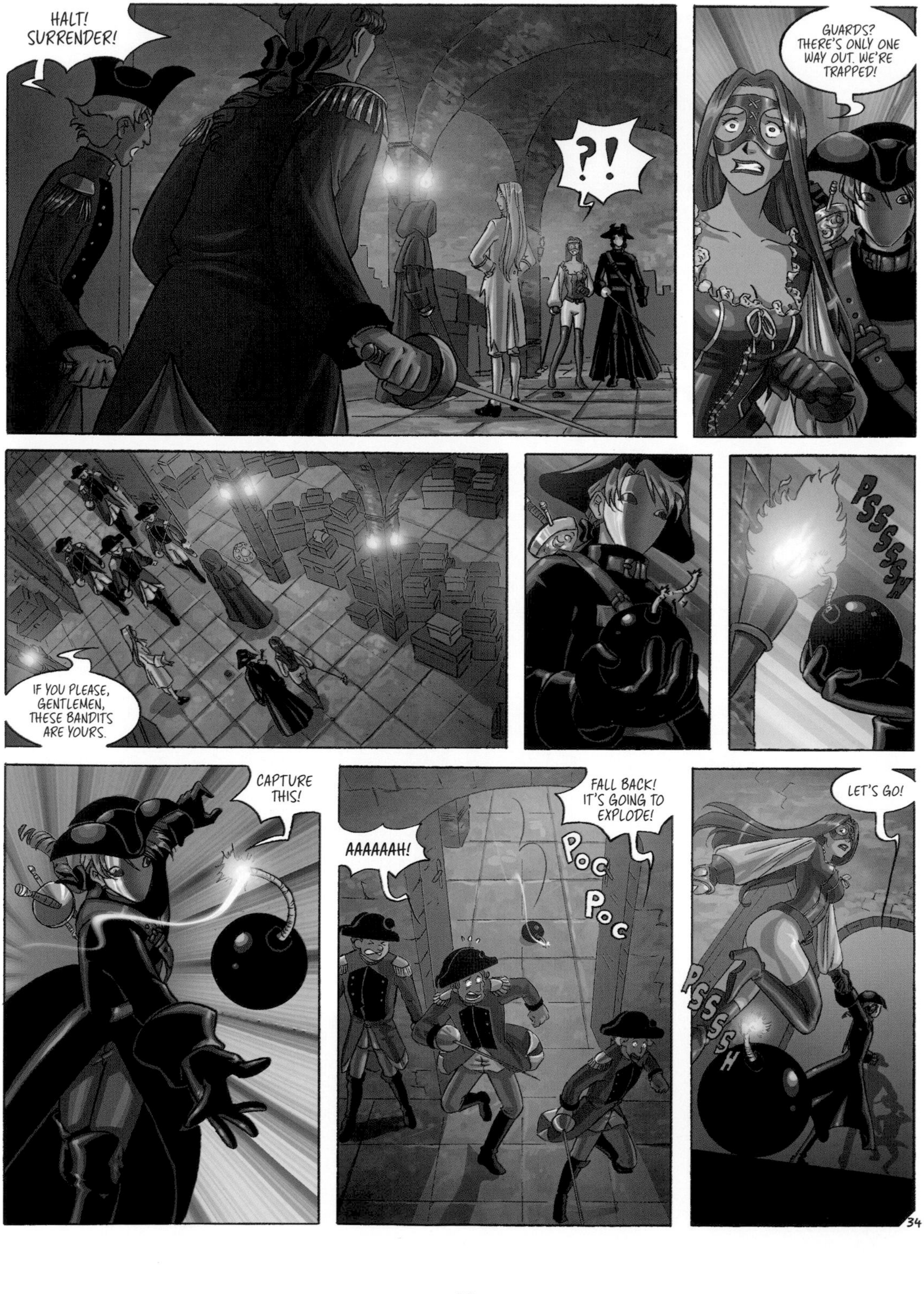
HALT! SURRENDER!
?!
GUARDS? THERE'S ONLY ONE WAY OUT. WE'RE TRAPPED!
IF YOU PLEASE, GENTLEMEN, THESE BANDITS ARE YOURS.
PSSSSSH
CAPTURE THIS!
FALL BACK! IT'S GOING TO EXPLODE!
AAAAAAH!
POC POC
LET'S GO!
PSSSSH
34

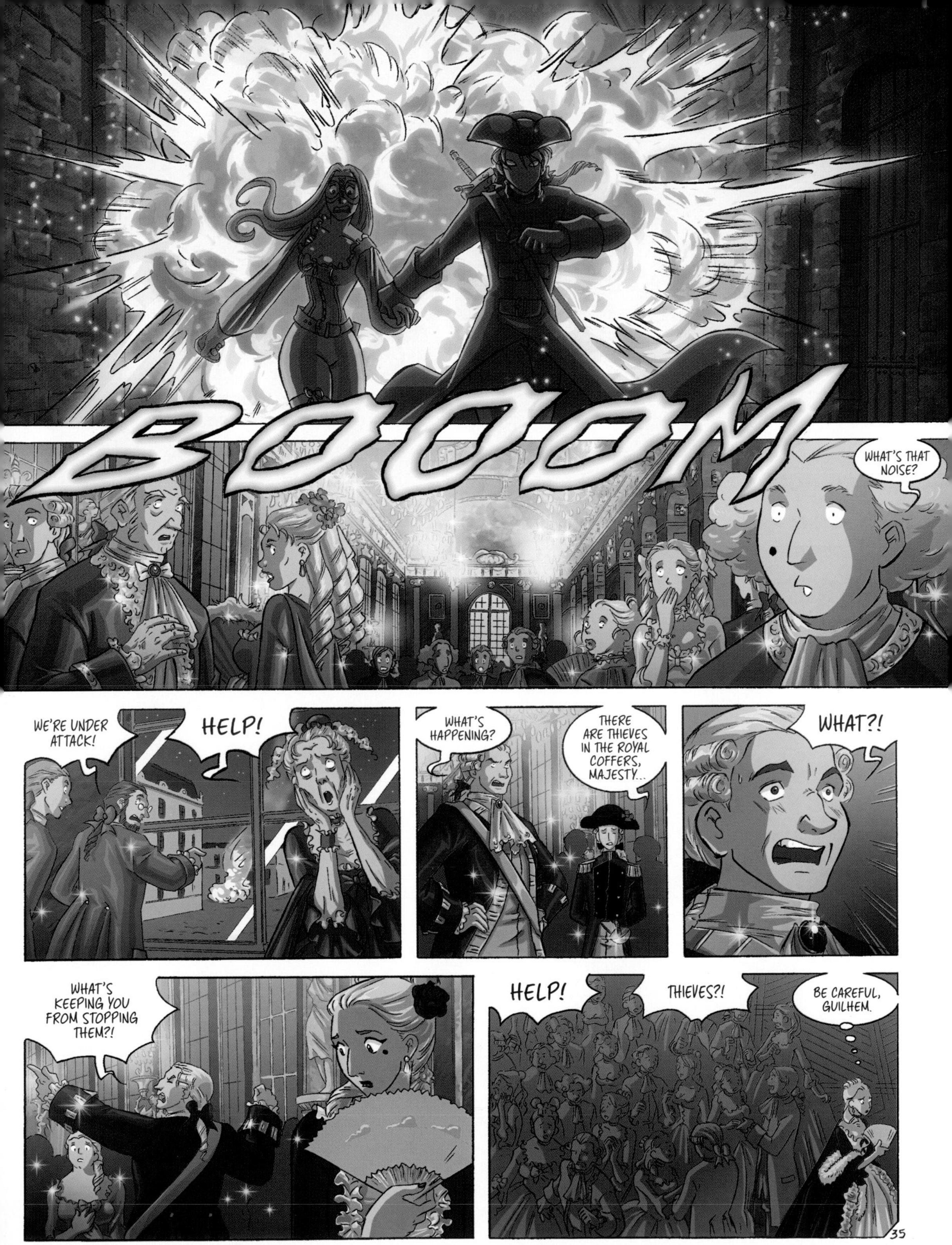
BOOOM
WHAT'S THAT NOISE?
WE'RE UNDER ATTACK!
HELP!
WHAT'S HAPPENING?
THERE ARE THIEVES IN THE ROYAL COFFERS, MAJESTY...
WHAT?!
WHAT'S KEEPING YOU FROM STOPPING THEM?!
HELP!
THIEVES?!
BE CAREFUL, GUILHEM.
35

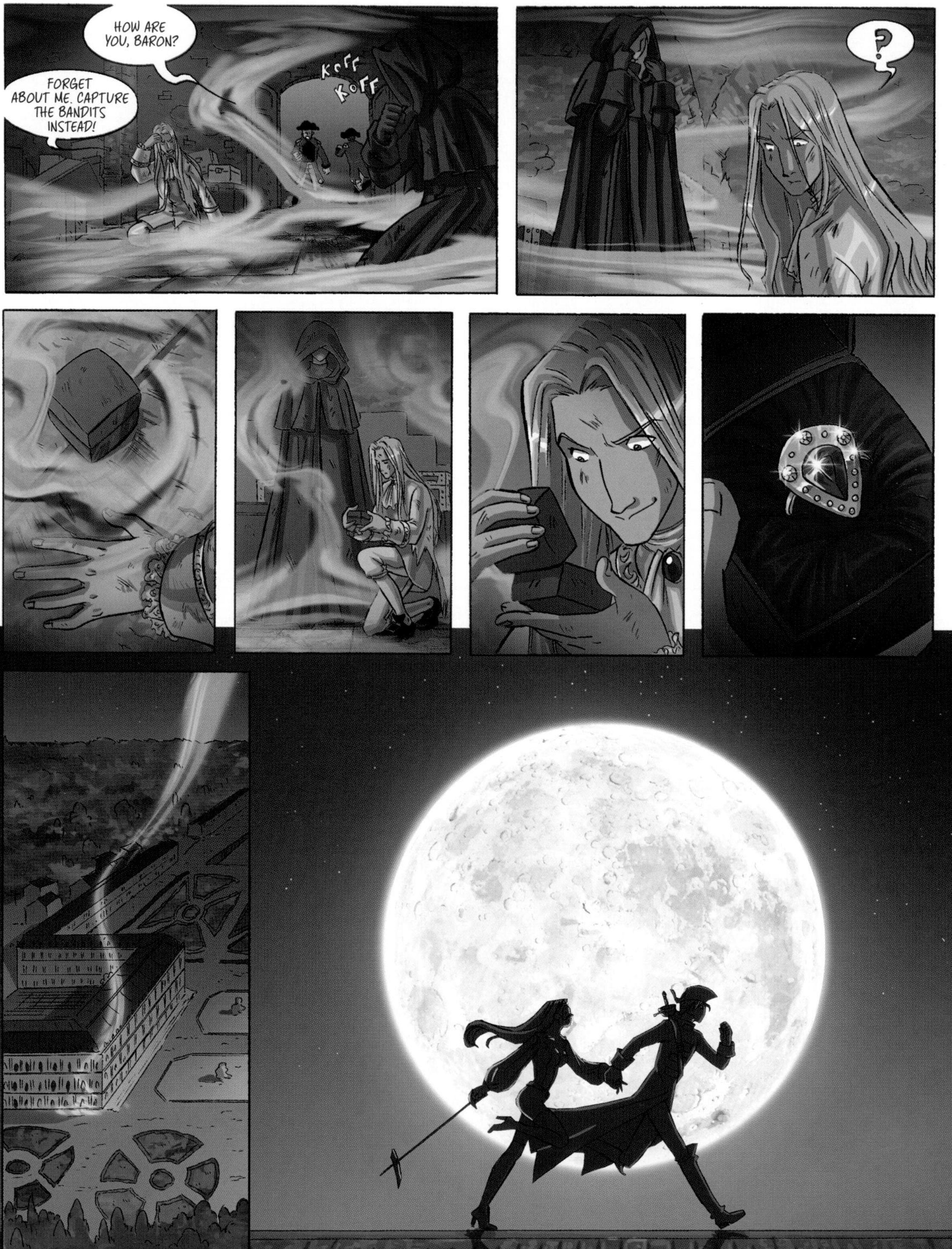

HOW ARE YOU, BARON?
FORGET ABOUT ME. CAPTURE THE BANDITS INSTEAD!
KOFF KOFF
?

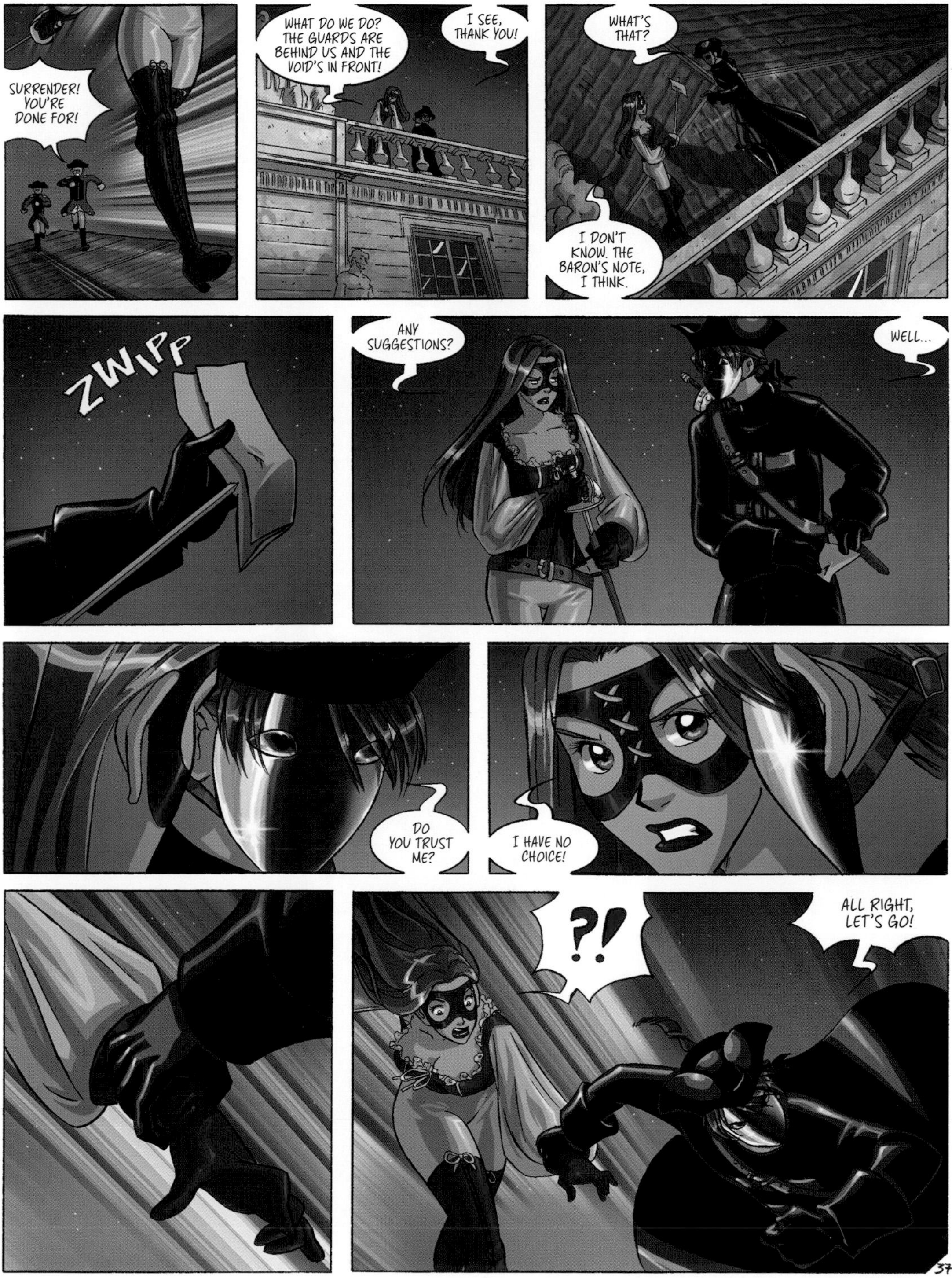
SURRENDER! YOU'RE DONE FOR!
WHAT DO WE DO? THE GUARDS ARE BEHIND US AND THE VOID'S IN FRONT!
I SEE, THANK YOU!
WHAT'S THAT?
I DON'T KNOW. THE BARON'S NOTE, I THINK.
ZWIPP
ANY SUGGESTIONS?
WELL...
DO YOU TRUST ME?
I HAVE NO CHOICE!
?!
ALL RIGHT, LET'S GO!
37

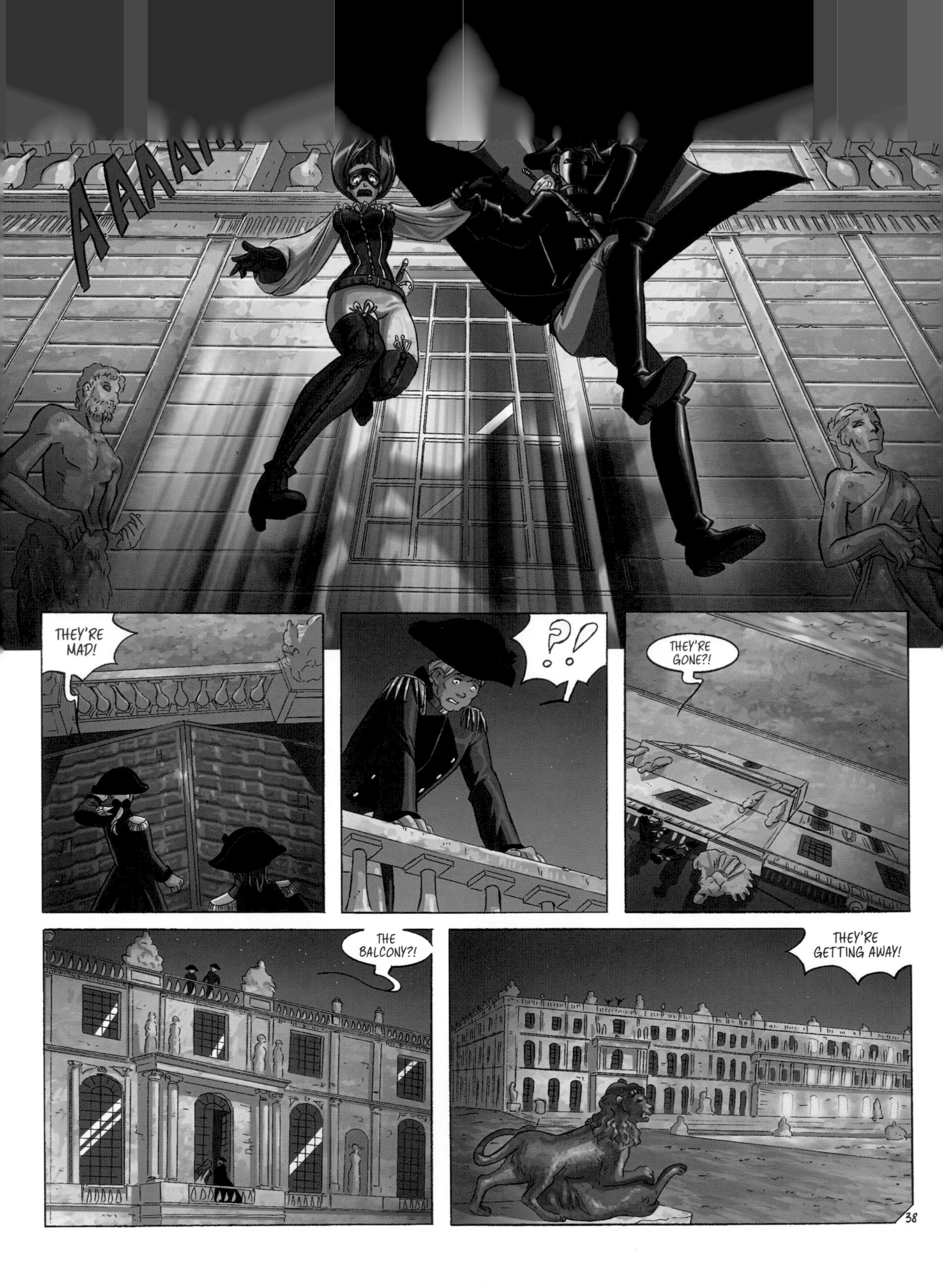

AAAAA
THEY'RE MAD!
?!
THEY'RE GONE?!
THE BALCONY?!
THEY'RE GETTING AWAY!
38

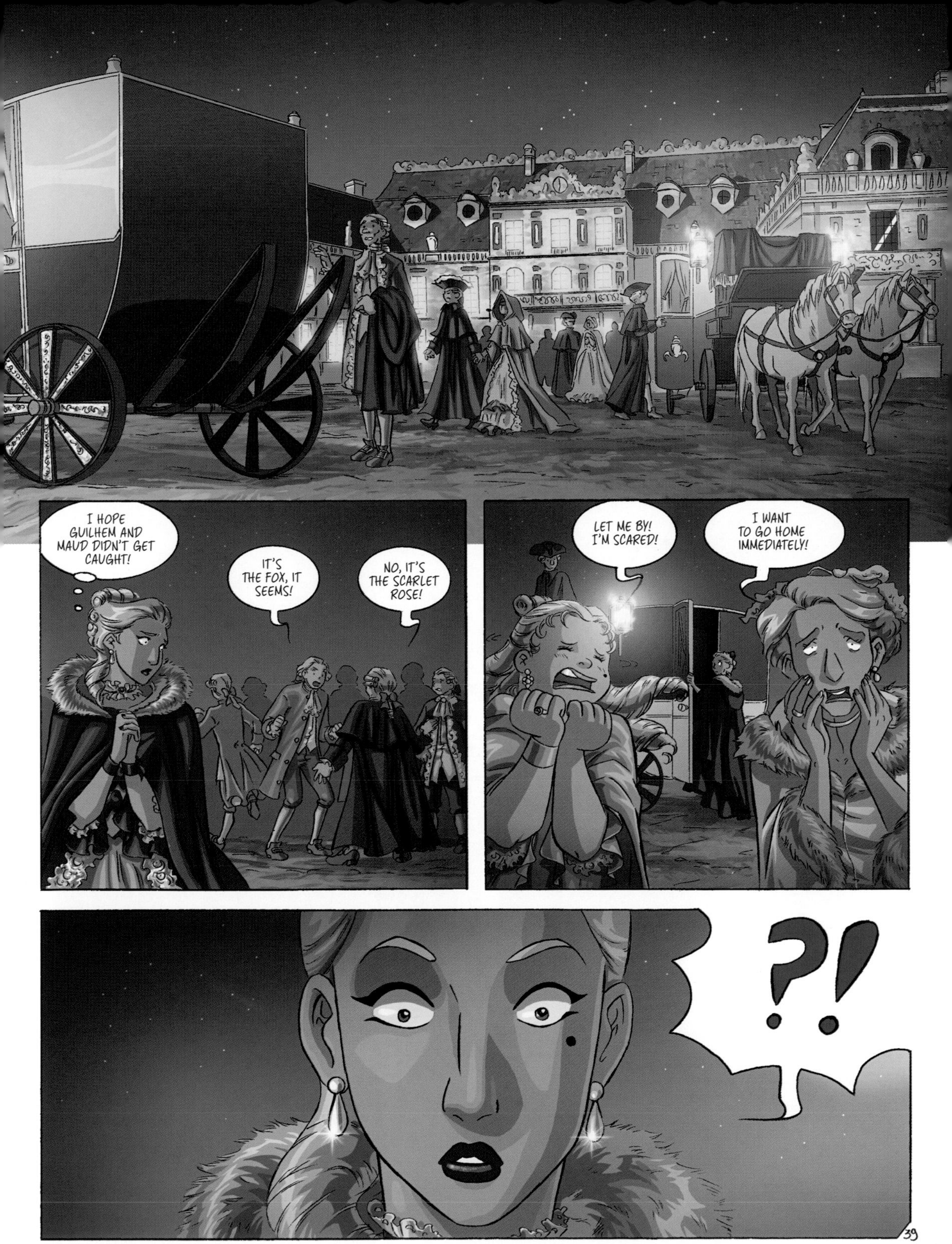
I HOPE GUILHEM AND MAUD DIDN'T GET CAUGHT!
IT'S THE FOX, IT SEEMS!
NO, IT'S THE SCARLET ROSE!
LET ME BY! I'M SCARED!
I WANT TO GO HOME IMMEDIATELY!
?!
39

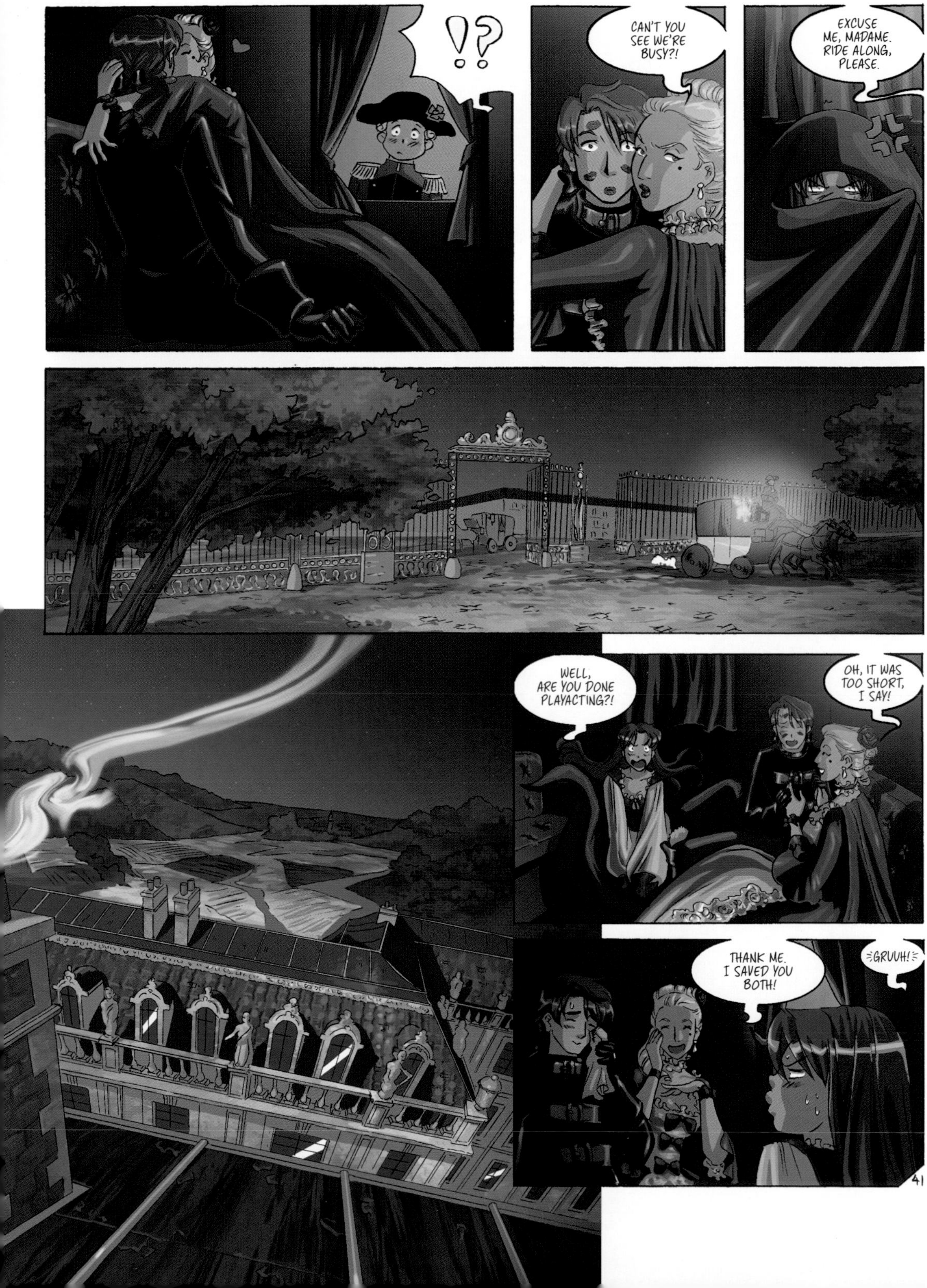
!?
CAN'T YOU SEE WE'RE BUSY?!
EXCUSE ME, MADAME. RIDE ALONG, PLEASE.
WELL, ARE YOU DONE PLAYACTING?!
OH, IT WAS TOO SHORT, I SAY!
THANK ME. I SAVED YOU BOTH!
GRUUH!

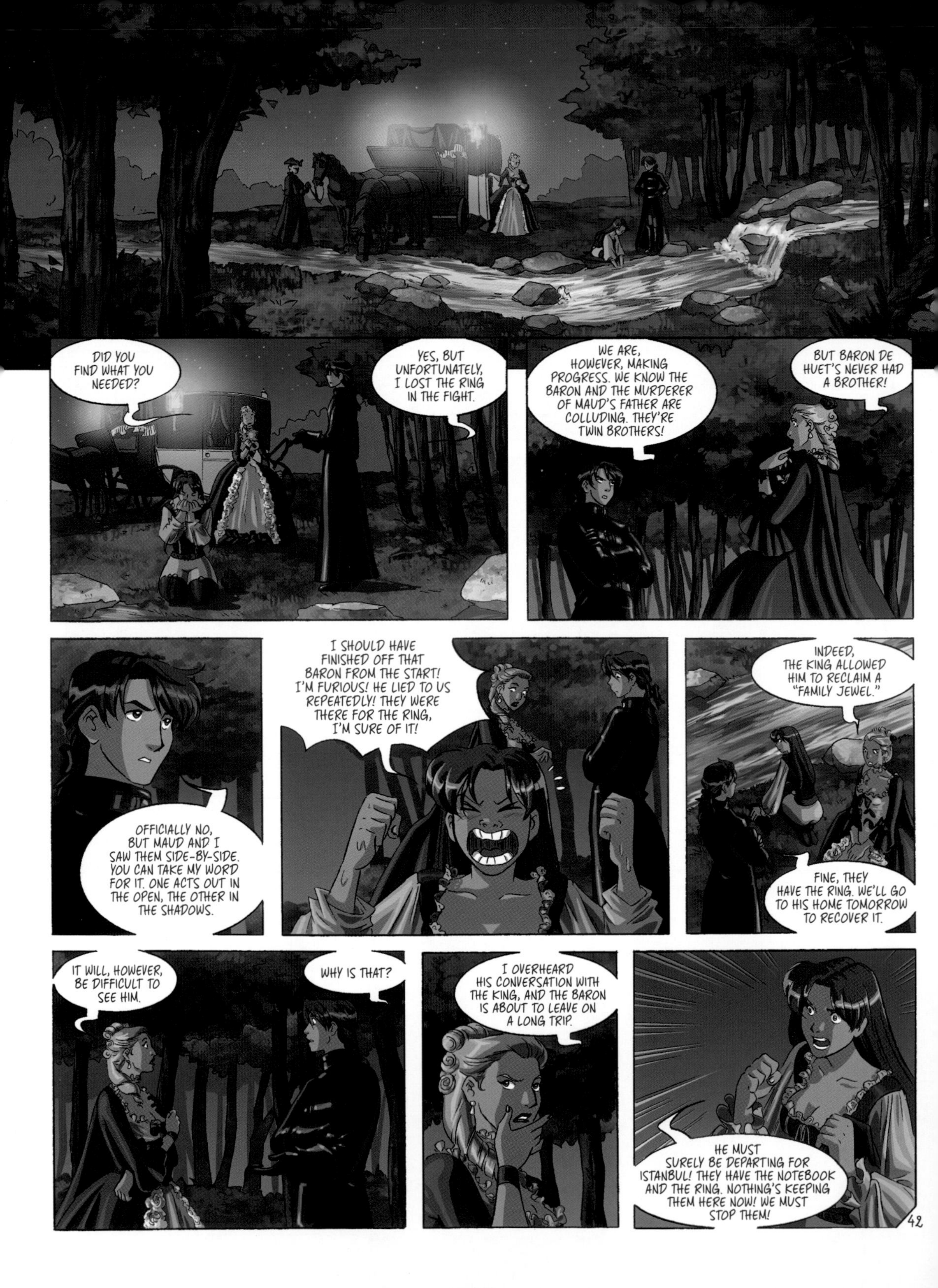
DID YOU FIND WHAT YOU NEEDED?
YES, BUT UNFORTUNATELY, I LOST THE RING IN THE FIGHT.
WE ARE, HOWEVER, MAKING PROGRESS. WE KNOW THE BARON AND THE MURDERER OF MAUD'S FATHER ARE COLLUDING. THEY'RE TWIN BROTHERS!
BUT BARON DE HUET'S NEVER HAD A BROTHER!
OFFICIALLY NO, BUT MAUD AND I SAW THEM SIDE-BY-SIDE. YOU CAN TAKE MY WORD FOR IT. ONE ACTS OUT IN THE OPEN, THE OTHER IN THE SHADOWS.
I SHOULD HAVE FINISHED OFF THAT BARON FROM THE START! I'M FURIOUS! HE LIED TO US REPEATEDLY! THEY WERE THERE FOR THE RING, I'M SURE OF IT!
INDEED, THE KING ALLOWED HIM TO RECLAIM A "FAMILY JEWEL."
FINE, THEY HAVE THE RING. WE'LL GO TO HIS HOME TOMORROW TO RECOVER IT.
IT WILL, HOWEVER, BE DIFFICULT TO SEE HIM.
WHY IS THAT?
I OVERHEARD HIS CONVERSATION WITH THE KING, AND THE BARON IS ABOUT TO LEAVE ON A LONG TRIP.
HE MUST SURELY BE DEPARTING FOR ISTANBUL! THEY HAVE THE NOTEBOOK AND THE RING. NOTHING'S KEEPING THEM HERE NOW! WE MUST STOP THEM!
42

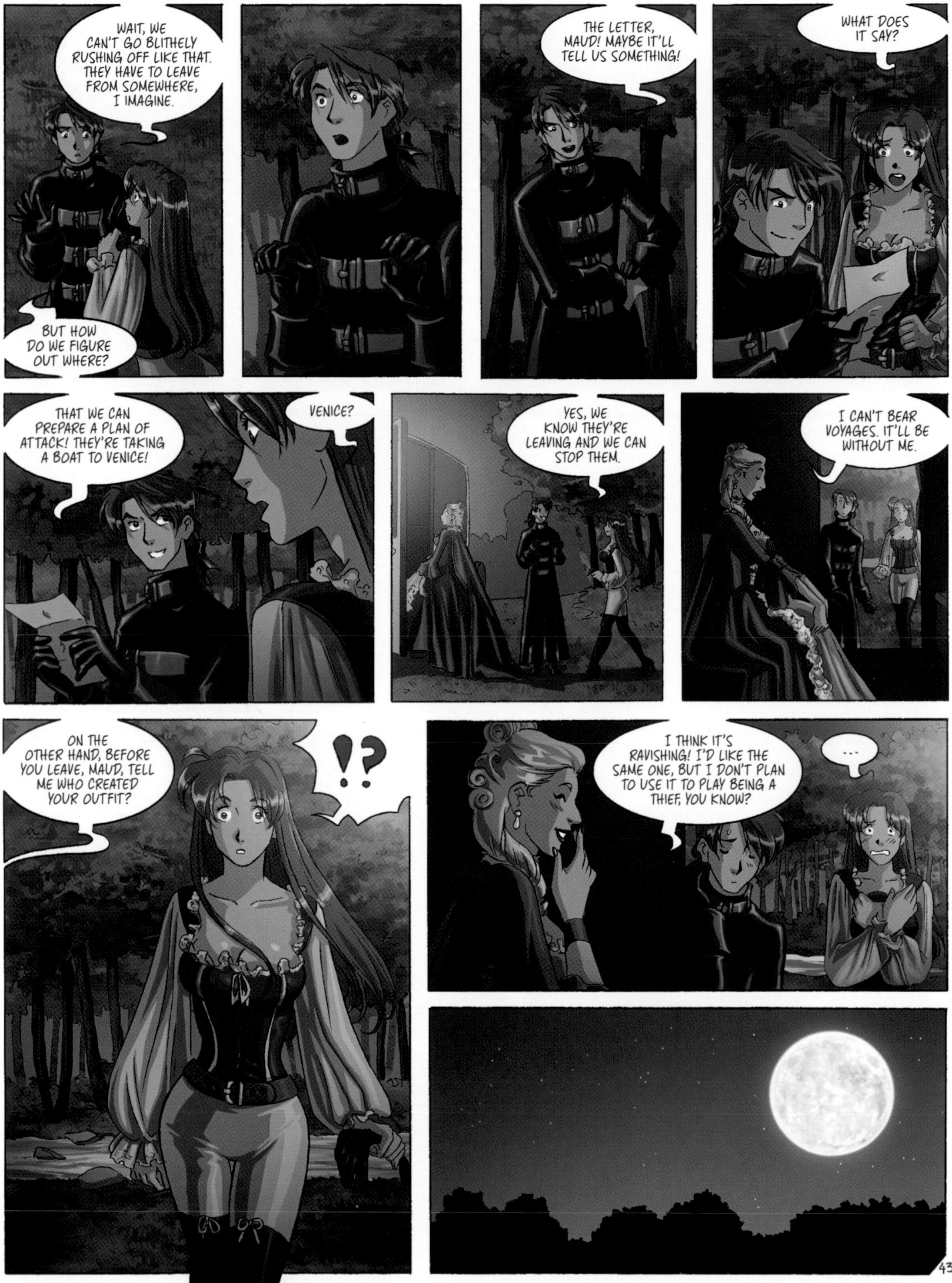
WAIT, WE CAN'T GO BLITHELY RUSHING OFF LIKE THAT. THEY HAVE TO LEAVE FROM SOMEWHERE, I IMAGINE.
BUT HOW DO WE FIGURE OUT WHERE?
THE LETTER, MAUD! MAYBE IT'LL TELL US SOMETHING!
WHAT DOES IT SAY?
THAT WE CAN PREPARE A PLAN OF ATTACK! THEY'RE TAKING A BOAT TO VENICE!
VENICE?
YES, WE KNOW THEY'RE LEAVING AND WE CAN STOP THEM.
I CAN'T BEAR VOYAGES. IT'LL BE WITHOUT ME.
ON THE OTHER HAND, BEFORE YOU LEAVE, MAUD, TELL ME WHO CREATED YOUR OUTFIT?
!?
I THINK IT'S RAVISHING! I'D LIKE THE SAME ONE, BUT I DON'T PLAN TO USE IT TO PLAY BEING A THIEF, YOU KNOW?
...
43

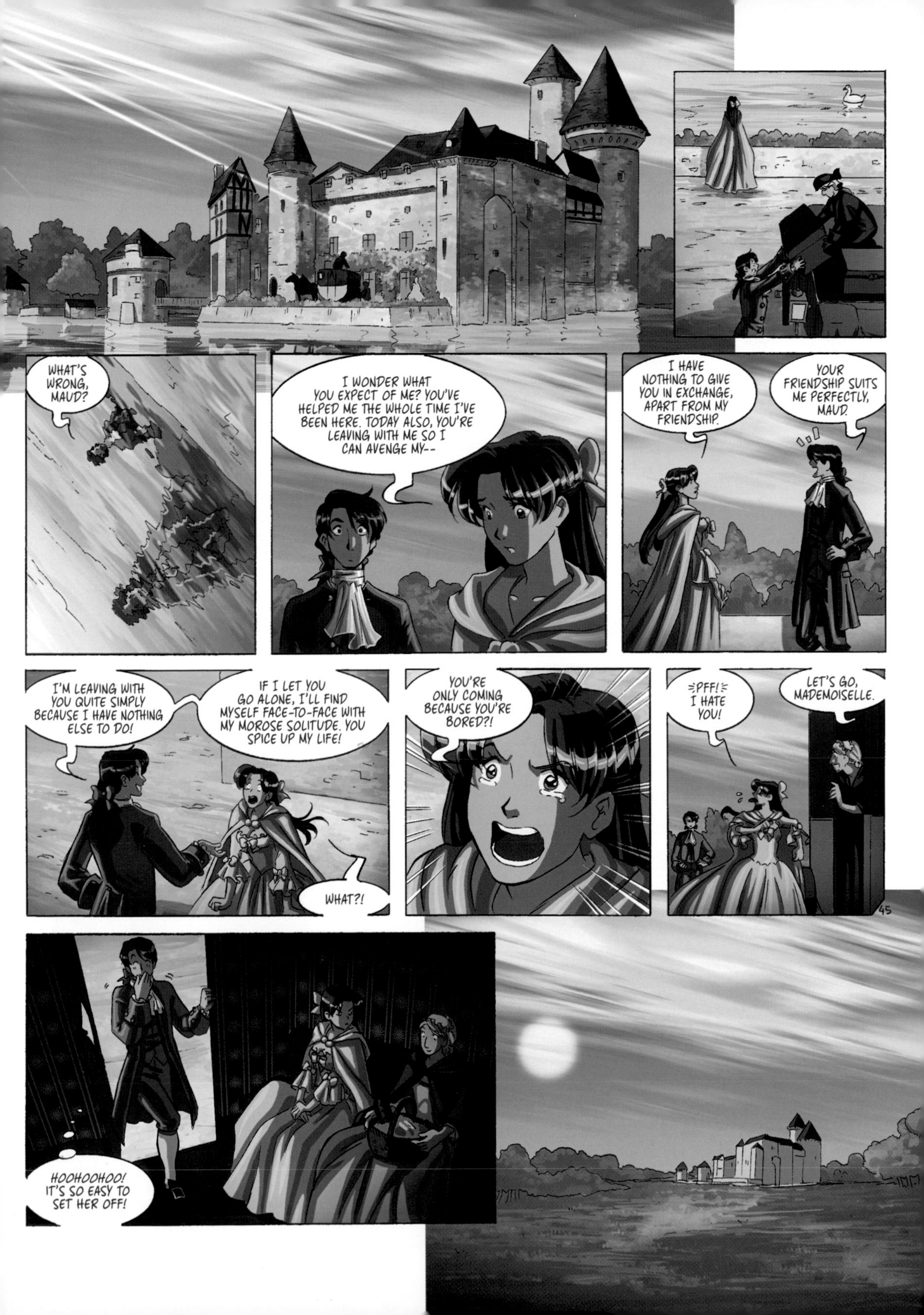

WHAT'S WRONG, MAUD?
I WONDER WHAT YOU EXPECT OF ME? YOU'VE HELPED ME THE WHOLE TIME I'VE BEEN HERE. TODAY ALSO, YOU'RE LEAVING WITH ME SO I CAN AVENGE MY--
I HAVE NOTHING TO GIVE YOU IN EXCHANGE, APART FROM MY FRIENDSHIP.
YOUR FRIENDSHIP SUITS ME PERFECTLY, MAUD.
I'M LEAVING WITH YOU QUITE SIMPLY BECAUSE I HAVE NOTHING ELSE TO DO!
IF I LET YOU GO ALONE, I'LL FIND MYSELF FACE-TO-FACE WITH MY MOROSE SOLITUDE. YOU SPICE UP MY LIFE!
WHAT?!
YOU'RE ONLY COMING BECAUSE YOU'RE BORED?!
PFF! I HATE YOU!
LET'S GO, MADEMOISELLE.
HOOHOOHOO! IT'S SO EASY TO SET HER OFF!

AND THAT'S HOW MAUD DE LAROCHE AND GUILHEM DE LANDREY CONTINUE THEIR WAY TO VENICE...

GRAZIE MILLE!*

...AND THE REPUTATION OF THE SCARLET ROSE AND THE FOX SPREAD BEYOND THE BORDERS OF FRANCE.

*ITALIAN : A THOUSAND THANKS.

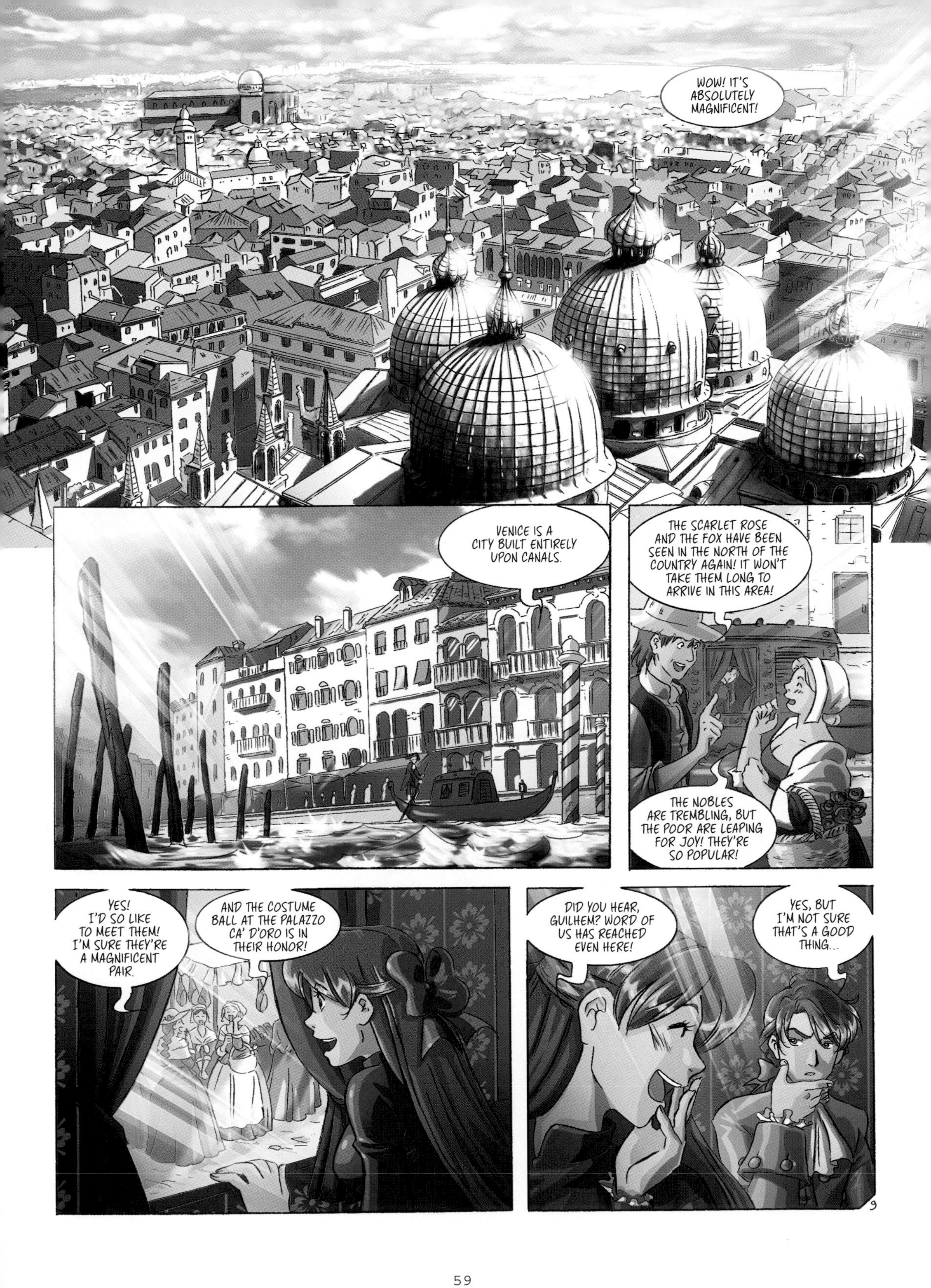
WOW! IT'S ABSOLUTELY MAGNIFICENT!
VENICE IS A CITY BUILT ENTIRELY UPON CANALS.
THE SCARLET ROSE AND THE FOX HAVE BEEN SEEN IN THE NORTH OF THE COUNTRY AGAIN! IT WON'T TAKE THEM LONG TO ARRIVE IN THIS AREA!
THE NOBLES ARE TREMBLING, BUT THE POOR ARE LEAPING FOR JOY! THEY'RE SO POPULAR!
YES! I'D SO LIKE TO MEET THEM! I'M SURE THEY'RE A MAGNIFICENT PAIR.
AND THE COSTUME BALL AT THE PALAZZO CA' D'ORO IS IN THEIR HONOR!
DID YOU HEAR, GUILHEM? WORD OF US HAS REACHED EVEN HERE!
YES, BUT I'M NOT SURE THAT'S A GOOD THING...
9

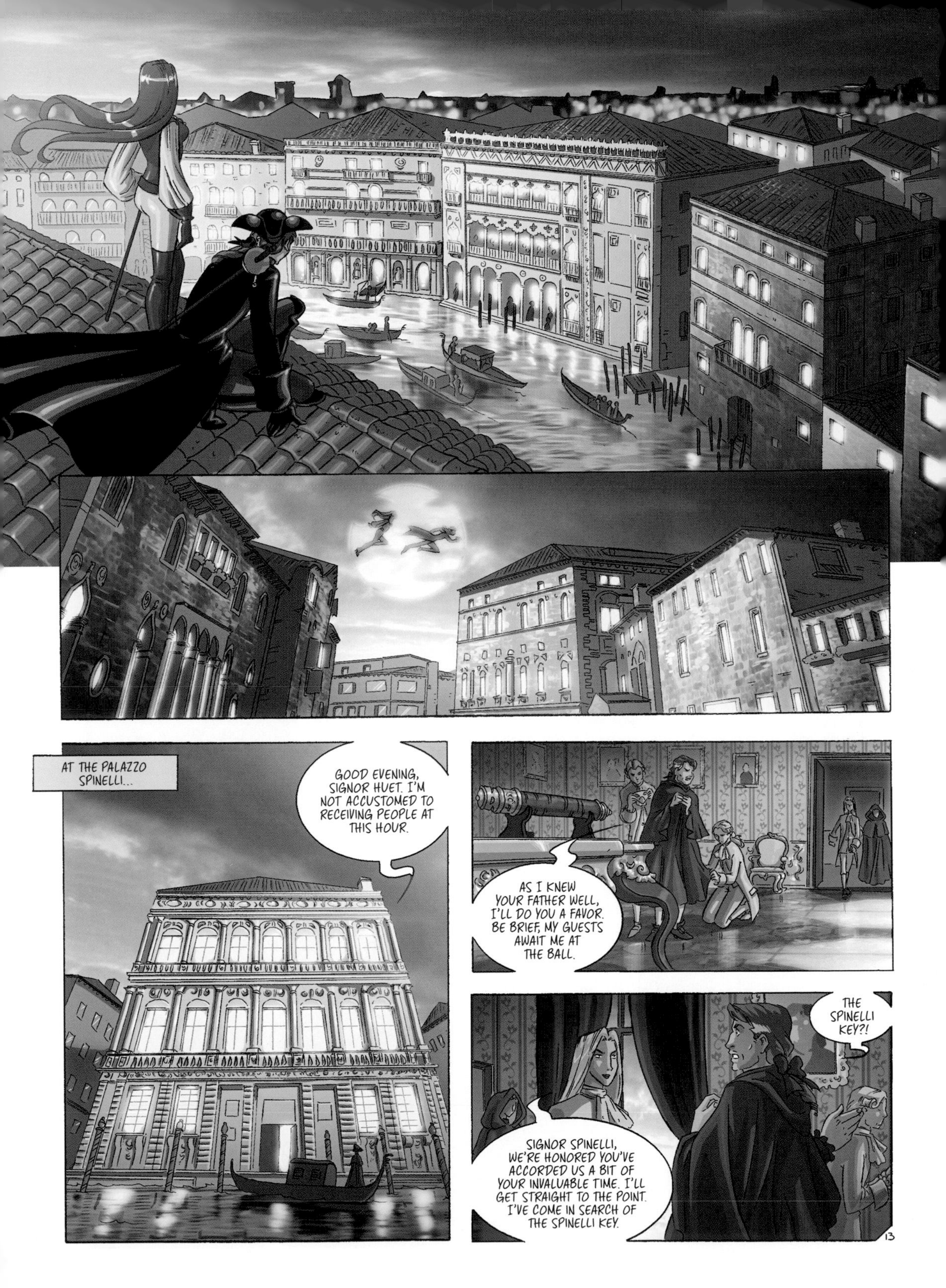
AT THE PALAZZO SPINELLI...
GOOD EVENING, SIGNOR HUET. I'M NOT ACCUSTOMED TO RECEIVING PEOPLE AT THIS HOUR.
AS I KNEW YOUR FATHER WELL, I'LL DO YOU A FAVOR. BE BRIEF, MY GUESTS AWAIT ME AT THE BALL.
SIGNOR SPINELLI, WE'RE HONORED YOU'VE ACCORDED US A BIT OF YOUR INVALUABLE TIME. I'LL GET STRAIGHT TO THE POINT. I'VE COME IN SEARCH OF THE SPINELLI KEY.
THE SPINELLI KEY?!
13

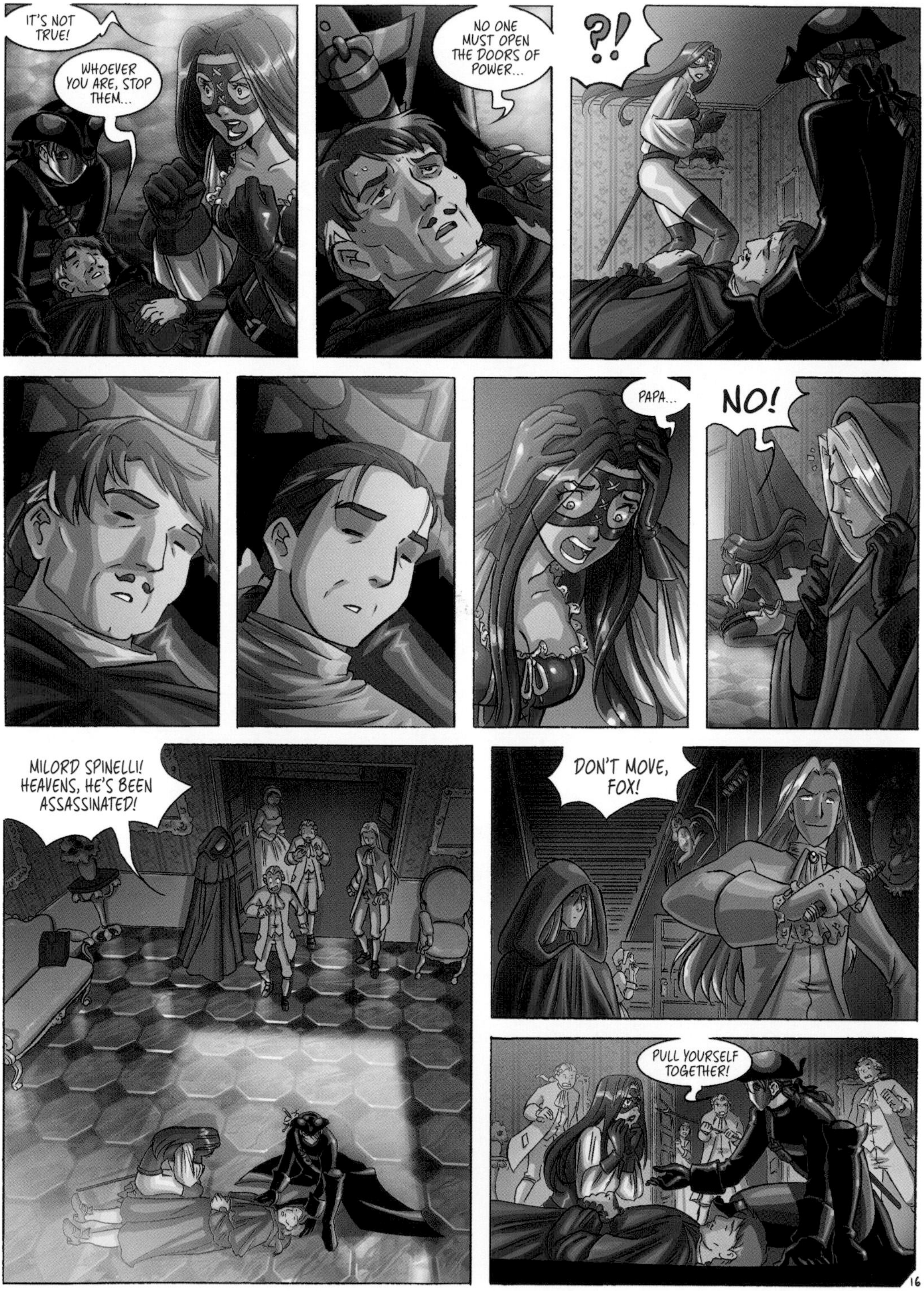
IT'S NOT TRUE!
WHOEVER YOU ARE, STOP THEM...
NO ONE MUST OPEN THE DOORS OF POWER...
?!
PAPA...
NO!
MILORD SPINELLI! HEAVENS, HE'S BEEN ASSASSINATED!
DON'T MOVE, FOX!
PULL YOURSELF TOGETHER!
16

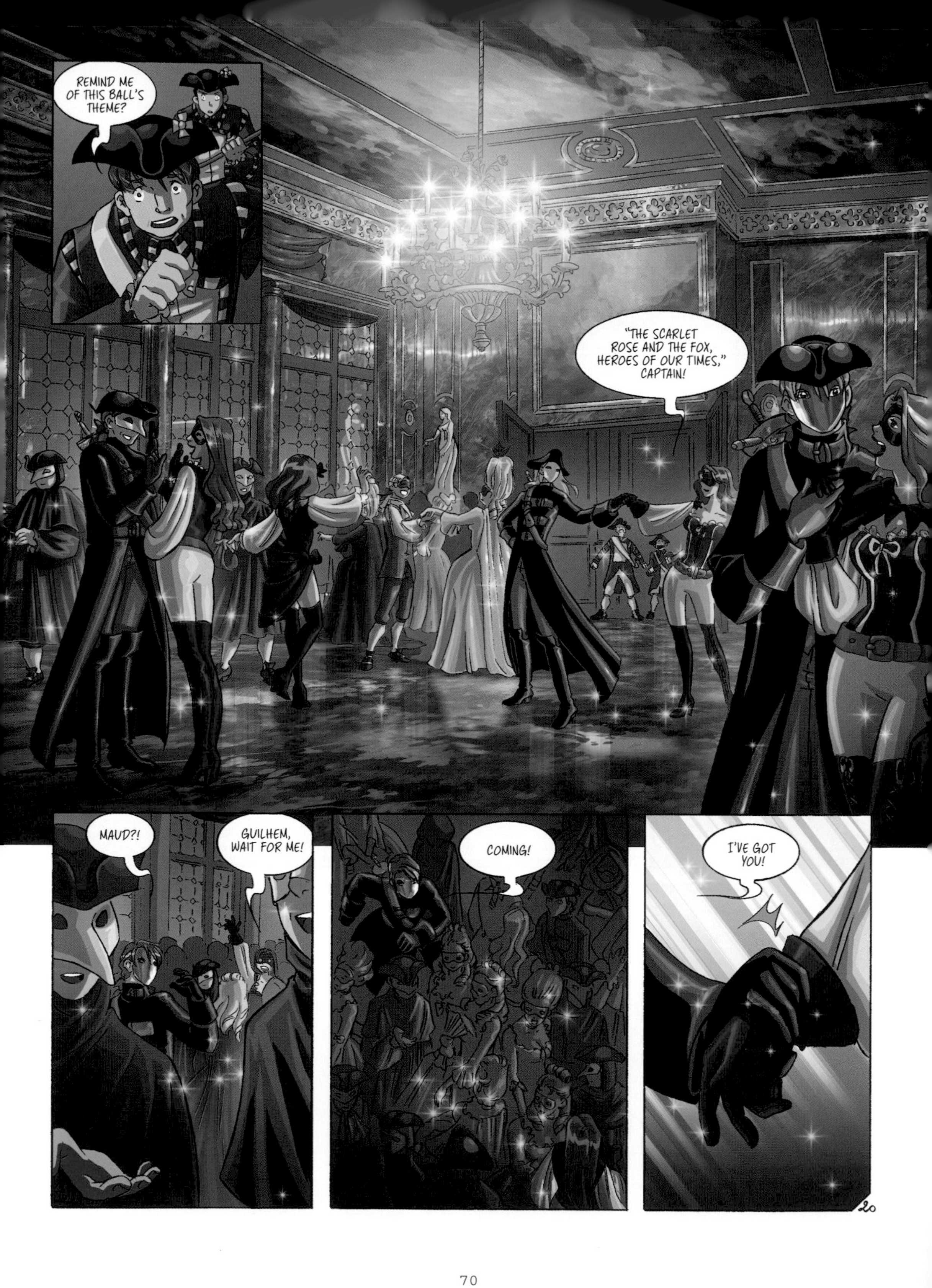
REMIND ME OF THIS BALL'S THEME?
"THE SCARLET ROSE AND THE FOX, HEROES OF OUR TIMES," CAPTAIN!
MAUD?!
GUILHEM, WAIT FOR ME!
COMING!
I'VE GOT YOU!
20

THAT SAME EVENING, AT THE PRISON OF VENICE...

EVENING, GENTLEMEN.

OH!

COULD WE KEEP YOU COMPANY? IT'S SO COLD HERE!

I'M SORRY, MA'AM, BUT WE'RE ON DUTY.

OH, YOU WON'T LEAVE TWO PRETTY, YOUNG WOMEN ALONE IN THE MIDDLE OF THE NIGHT?

IS SHE OVERDOING IT?

OH...

ALL RIGHT THEN, JUST A GLASS!

HEE HEE HEE!

YIKES! I'VE CAUGHT THE GORILLA'S EYE!

COME ON, WE'LL JUST OFFER THEM A SMALL GLASS OF WINE! I THINK THE ONE ON THE RIGHT'S SO BEAUTIFUL!